"Come with me."

Nicole took Ian's hand and led him down to the beach, to a hammock strung between two palm trees.

"Lie down," she commanded, and pushed him into the hammock.

He did as told, and Nicole crawled on top of him and straddled his stomach. She planted her palms on his chest and stared down at him, her expression serious.

"Yes or no?" she asked. "Do you want to be seduced?"

Heat rushed through her—the heat of desire, and also a great sensation of power. With her eyes locked with his, she reached up, grasped the top of her dress and lowered the silky fabric over her breasts—slowly, revealing an inch of naked skin at a time and watching as Ian's eyes darkened with desire.

"Yes," he whispered. "Absolutely yes."

Blaze™

Dear Reader,

I had a thing for pirates long before Johnny Depp and Orlando Bloom made them popular. As a girl, I devoured stories about Blackbeard, Captain Kidd and Jean Lafitte. And as I grew older, I fantasized about being swept off my feet by a dashing pirate and carried away to a tropical paradise. (It beats figuring my taxes or making a grocery list any day of the week.)

That tropical paradise of my dreams seemed the perfect setting for a pair of sexy Harlequin Blaze fantasies. Add in the lure of treasure and legends about pirates and this was a story I couldn't wait to return to every day. Better than Blackbeard or Captain Kidd, I made my pirate a woman with a scandalous past and a reputation as a skilled seductress. I pulled out all the stops for the character of Passionata, and I hope you'll enjoy the steamy results.

Look for the second Passionata's Island story in October 2008, when *Her Secret Treasure* goes on sale. In the meantime, I love to hear from my readers. You'll find me on the Web at www.CindiMyers.com. E-mail me at cindi@cindimyers.com or write to me in care of Harlequin Enterprises, 225 Duncan Mill Road, Don Mills, Ontario M3B 3K9, Canada.

Best,

Cindi Myers

AT HER PLEASURE
Cindi Myers

HARLEQUIN®

TORONTO • NEW YORK • LONDON
AMSTERDAM • PARIS • SYDNEY • HAMBURG
STOCKHOLM • ATHENS • TOKYO • MILAN • MADRID
PRAGUE • WARSAW • BUDAPEST • AUCKLAND

ISBN-13: 978-0-373-79423-2
ISBN-10:   0-373-79423-1

AT HER PLEASURE

Copyright © 2008 by Cynthia Myers.

ABOUT THE AUTHOR

Cindi Myers's dreams of sailing away to an island paradise with her own swashbuckling pirate have been quashed by rampant seasickness and a tendency to sunburn easily. So she settles for drinking umbrella cocktails and letting her imagination run wild on the sun-washed beaches of her books.

Books by Cindi Myers

To Emily McKay, for all her help
in researching diving.
Any mistakes are mine, not hers.

1

THE SUNSET ON THE OCEAN streaked the sky with pink and gold and turned the sea a deep vermillion.

The color of passion.

The color of romance and love and all the things that weren't a part of Nicole Howard's life right now. And maybe never would be again.

She leaned on the rail of the yacht and stared out at a horizon as empty and featureless as she felt inside. Maybe agreeing to come on this vacation with her friend, Adam Carroway, hadn't been such a great idea.

With his usual persuasiveness, Adam had made the trip sound like the perfect way to recover from losing both her lover and her job in the space of a week. They'd sail to a remote island in the Caribbean, do some diving, look for some shipwreck Adam was wild to find, get some sun and forget all about life back in Amity, Michigan.

But forgetting was proving a lot harder than Nicole had expected.

"You're thinking about him again, aren't you? Stop it."

She turned and saw Adam emerging from the ship's cabin. Broad-shouldered, barrel-chested and tanned from hours sailing on Lake Michigan, he looked nothing like the university history professor he was. Ten years older than Nicole, he had been at various times her roommate, confidant and best buddy. She thought of him as the big brother she'd never had.

He came to stand beside her on the rail. "You should have let me pound him one. Then at least you'd have the memory of him groveling to cheer you up."

She shook her head. She couldn't imagine Dr. Kenneth Brambling, chief of Amity Surgical Associates, groveling. When she'd first taken the job as nurse for the busy surgery practice, she'd been intimidated by his dignity. Later, when they'd become lovers, she'd been caught up in the aura of power with which he surrounded himself.

Only recently had she realized Kenneth's dignity was merely arrogance, and the power an inflated sense of his own importance, and a callousness that had shocked her—and broken her heart. "Beating him up wouldn't have gotten either of us anything except maybe a lawsuit," she said.

"Might have made him think twice about cheating on another woman."

"I doubt it." As soon as she'd gotten over the shock of learning that she wasn't the only woman sharing Kenneth's bed, she'd uncovered all sorts of deceptions the good doctor excelled in, from exaggerating reports to insurance companies in order to receive higher reimbursements, to lying to his partners about the real reason he couldn't attend a staff meeting—because he'd been occupied with his latest girlfriend. The man was an accomplished liar and it was cold comfort to know she wasn't the first fool he'd deceived.

She'd emerged from the affair doubting everything from her physical attractiveness to her judgment. Though she knew Kenneth was in the wrong—he was the one who'd cheated and lied—she couldn't help but wonder if she was also to blame. Maybe if she'd handled things differently, she wouldn't have ended up so hurt.

"Here, I brought you something to take your mind off the jerk." Adam pulled a slim paperback from his pocket and offered it to her.

"What is it?"

"Some background info on where we're going and what I hope to find there."

Adam had tried previously to give her more details about their destination and the shipwreck he was searching for, but once he went into academic-lecture mode her eyes glazed over and she'd refused to listen further. She didn't care *why* they were headed to this deserted island, only that the island was far from Michigan and her problems.

Expecting a boring academic tome, she took the book and studied the cover. A lurid watercolor portrayed a scantily clad woman standing on a gallows. *Confessions of a Pirate Queen?* she read the title, amused. This certainly didn't sound like a textbook.

"Passionata, aka Jane Hallowell, was a female pirate in the early 1700s, based on a previously deserted atoll that came to be known as Passionata's Island—our destination on this trip," said Adam.

"A female pirate?" This definitely piqued her interest. "Were there really such things?"

"Definitely. The most well-known is Anne Bonney, but there's also Mary Reade, and Grace O'Malley, the daughter of a pirate who followed in her father's footsteps." He tapped the cover of the book. "But Passionata was in a class by herself."

Nicole turned the volume over and studied the painting of a full-rigged sailing ship with a Jolly Roger flying from its mast. "How so?"

"For one thing, she was one of the most successful. She and her all-female crew liberated merchant ships—mostly British— of millions of dollars in cargo, from gold coins to imported spices." Adam had warmed to his subject now, assuming the tone of a professor lecturing his students.

"I guess that kind of money will get you talked about," Nicole said.

"It wasn't only the money people talked about." He grinned. "Passionata had an interesting approach to life."

As if being a female pirate wasn't interesting enough.

"She was known as quite a seductress, and advocated ideas that were shocking for their time. Supposedly some of the highest members of British society secretly came to the island, seeking her advice on the art of seduction."

Nicole studied the cover illustration again. "So is this one of those tabloid tell-alls about her sordid life?"

"This book was supposedly written by Passionata herself while she was awaiting trial in Newgate Prison in 1715." He tapped the cover again. "Read it. I think you'll find it interesting."

She nodded. She'd brought a couple of novels with her, but none of them had been able to hold her interest. What she really needed was something to help her get over the failures she'd left behind. She could approach *Confessions of a Pirate Queen* like one of those self-help books everyone swore by. A woman who'd succeeded in a male-dominated field might have some handy career lessons to impart, and a pirate queen who was also a known seductress could surely teach Nicole a few things about charting her own course in her relationships with men. She lay back against the pillows in the narrow bunk in the ship's cabin and read the opening lines with interest:

I, PASSIONATA, the most famous lady pirate, stand as a witness to the power of woman. It is this strength that has made the men who govern the laws of the land tremble in fear before me. It is this mastery and my audacity in using it that has led them to seek to silence me on the gallows. But as long as I have breath I will speak, so that others, women and men, may learn.

I am Passionata, and this is my truth.

What exactly did the lady pirate mean about "the power of woman"? Weren't women of her day more powerless than most? As much as Nicole could recall from her college history courses, in those days women weren't allowed to own property or sign legal documents. They were at the mercy of their husbands or male relatives.

Things had changed a great deal for the better, but she had to admit that one of the things that had hurt most in the whole debacle with Kenneth had been her own feeling of powerlessness. He had held all the cards. When she'd learned of his infidelity and lies, she'd wept and ranted and made demands—all of which he ignored with an unsettling calmness that only made her feel more out of control.

Then he'd fired her, and there'd been nothing she could do. He'd pointed out—also with chilling calm—that as owner of the business he had the right to hire and fire anyone he wished, at any time, for any reason. Besides, he'd added, everyone knew about their affair and that it had ended, and she didn't want to stay around to become the object of office gossip, did she?

Ha! Too bad she didn't have the option of turning pirate and making Dr. Ken walk the plank!

I was born Jane Hallowell, daughter of George Hallowell, a successful merchant, owner of a half-dozen fine merchant ships. I was no great beauty as a child, but as I matured I was endowed with a handsomeness that attracted men.

One of these men was a pirate. His name does not matter here, and indeed, I have vowed never to speak it again. He wooed me with pretty presents and exciting tales of his adventures on the seas. He mesmerized me with smooth words and aroused in me feelings I had never experienced before. He stole my virtue—nay, I gave it gladly, knowing that I was in love and one day would soon wed.

What a naive child I was! On the very day when I waited on the docks for my lover to arrive and take me away with him forever, I learned that my father's fleet of merchant ships had been attacked, and had suffered a grievous loss. My poor father wailed and buried his face in his hands. When I asked who had done this thing, he uttered the very name of my pirate!

The man I had loved, to whom I had given my all, had never loved me. He had used me to learn the secrets of my father's business—the routes of my father's ships and their cargos. He had struck like a cobra, taking all, destroying my father.

Destroying me.

Or so he thought. But I would not be destroyed. Not when the creditors came to auction the house and all our belongings. Not when my father took his own life by shooting himself with a pistol. I died, too, then. Jane Hallowell died.

But Passionata was born.

Fascinated, Nicole read on. She learned how Passionata took her father's last remaining ship and sailed to the pirate's haven of Tortuga, where she searched among the brothels and bars for other women like herself—desperate women with nothing to lose and a determination to take revenge on the male sex who had used them so cruelly. From one of the women she learned of the deserted atoll where she made her headquarters and began almost sixteen years of seduction and destruction.

Yes, we were women. The so-called weaker sex, without the physical strength of men. But we have something greater. We have the mental stamina that only women have.

And we have the one weapon that can bring all men to their knees. For every man—as long as he is a true man, and not the other kind, who, indeed I have found to be great allies—will succumb to the power of a woman's sexuality. Since Adam bowed before Eve, men have always been defeated by this power.

I have devoted my life to teaching all women who want to learn how to use this power. A woman who knows the power of her own body will never be at the mercy of a mere man again.

Nicole reread these last words out loud. "'A woman who knows the power of her own body will never be at the mercy of a mere man again.'" *A man like Kenneth,* she thought.

She eagerly turned to the next chapter in Passionata's tale. Adam had told her she'd enjoy the book, but he probably hadn't anticipated she would take it so much to heart.

For the first time since cleaning out her desk at the surgical center, she began to feel hope. This book—and this vacation on the island where Passionata had made her home—was Nicole's opportunity to start fresh. She'd devote this time to learning what the lady pirate had to teach her, and she would never be "at the mercy of a mere man again."

IAN MARSHALL MOVED THROUGH the packed marketplace in Ocho Rios, Jamaica, easing around clots of T-shirt-clad tourists and craning his neck to see into the vendors' stalls, while at the same time trying not to appear too interested.

"Come and see. I have nice souvenirs for you." A man with Rastafarian dreadlocks motioned him toward a table of wood carvings.

Ian shook his head and backed away. The vendor picked up a carving and advanced toward him. "You like a little smoke? A little ganja? I have a lighter for you." He slid down a panel at the bottom of the carving of a man and revealed an oversize penis-shaped lighter.

Ian shook his head and darted away, only to collide with a tableful of straw baskets. "You want to buy a basket?" the woman asked, never missing a beat as she straightened her wares. "Very beautiful. Very useful."

Ian stopped to consider the baskets. He could probably use something like this, to store food or collect specimens. And he *had* almost upset her stall. He picked up a large round basket. "How much for this one?" he asked.

She named a price that sounded more than reasonable. He quickly paid her and moved on. He didn't have much time and he still had a long list of supplies to obtain. He was going to be on the island for three months and had to take with him everything he'd need to survive. The guide at the wharf had told them there was a surplus store near here that could outfit him, and he'd cut through this market thinking it was a short cut.

Bad idea. He couldn't move two steps without someone imploring him to come inside their stall and "Just look." And every minute he lingered here was costing him. He'd agreed to be back in two hours to board the merchant ship on which he'd booked passage. They would drop him off on the island in the morning. If he didn't show up, they wouldn't hesitate to sail without him, and his work would be delayed.

Up ahead, past the cluster of stalls, he spotted part of a large overhead marquis. Could that be the place he was looking for? Head down, he moved as swiftly as he dared through the crowd, deaf now to the cries of the vendors.

A dark hand reached out and grabbed hold of him. When he tried to shake it off, the fingers tightened around his arm.

"You don't want to pass up what I am offering," said a honey-smooth voice.

Annoyed, he glanced to his right and found himself staring into a pair of intense black eyes. They belonged to a woman wearing a red and yellow headscarf. Her face was smooth and unlined, but those eyes looked as if they'd seen a lot. "Come in here," she said, pulling him toward her stall. "I have something for you."

"No, really, I don't have time—"

But already they were at the door of the little shack that served as her shop. "You will not regret making time for this." She reached up to a shelf and chose a small blue glass bottle and pressed it into his hand.

The shack was filled with such bottles, in every color of the rainbow. He stared down at the one she'd handed him. It had no label, but he could see it was three-quarters full of some dark liquid. "What is this?"

She smiled, showing large, yellowed teeth. "It is a love potion. You put some in the drink of a woman you desire and she will be unable to resist you."

He wondered if it would have worked on Danielle, his most recent ex-girlfriend. She'd certainly found him easy to resist. When he'd suggested she accompany him on this trip, she'd actually laughed in his face. "You're going off to some deserted island to play Robinson Crusoe for three months? You won't last a week." She'd patted him on the shoulder, a patronizing gesture that had enraged him, though he'd kept his emotions in check. "Ian, the only things you know about life you learned from books. You live in your head, not the real world. But I'm out here where real life is happening. I want a man who can be there with me."

"Let me guess, you've already found him," he'd said.

She didn't seem to notice his sarcasm. "I've found a real man who makes me happy," she said.

Doctoral students who spent most of their time in research libraries and classrooms didn't qualify as authentic males, apparently.

One more reason to take this trip. He'd spend the summer living by his wits, relying only on his own labor and strength. He'd prove to Danielle—and to himself—that he had brains *and* brawn. That he was a *real* man.

So what would Danielle think if she could see him now, being bullied by shop venders?

He shoved the bottle back at the woman. "I don't need any love potions," he said. "There aren't any women where I'll be spending my summer."

She narrowed her eyes, then grabbed his wrist in an iron grip and drew his hand toward her, palm up. She lowered her face until her nose was almost touching his skin and stared. He tried to pull away, but he might as well have been trying to free himself from a bear trap.

The woman raised her head and looked into his eyes. "No, you won't need a love potion. But I have something else you *will* need." She dropped his hand, whirled and chose another bottle from the shelf.

This small flask was purple, and was warm against his skin when she pressed it into his hand.

"What is it?" he asked.

She grinned again. "Drink this and you will be able to make love to any woman for hours. You will stay harder and larger and will give her pleasure like she has never known."

He almost dropped the bottle, and felt his face grow hot. "Um, I don't think I'll need this, either." No woman had ever complained about his, um, *stamina* before. "I told you, there aren't any women where I'm going."

"You are wrong. There is a woman in your future," she said. "A seductress whose goal will be to wear you out." She tapped the bottle with a long, painted nail. "With this, you will never wear out."

A pair of tourists had entered the shop and were staring at him with open interest, obviously hearing every word the woman was saying. Ian pulled out his wallet, desperate to get rid of her. "How much?" he asked.

"Ten dollar," she said. "Worth every penny."

Ten dollars was robbery, but he paid it, anxious to be out of there and on his way. He shoved the bottle deep into his backpack, then ran the rest of the way toward the surplus store.

He told himself it was only his imagination that he could feel the woman's eyes burning into his back as he escaped.

THE NEXT MORNING OVER breakfast, Adam asked Nicole if she'd had a bad night.

She yawned and stirred sugar into her coffee. "Why do you say that?"

He helped himself to a second bagel and began slathering it with cream cheese. "You don't look as if you slept well."

"I was up late reading."

He smirked. "About Passionata?"

She nodded. "If she did even half the things she said she did, she was amazing."

"Supposedly it's all true, though I have my doubts."

She sipped her coffee and studied him over the rim of her cup. Adam wouldn't believe anything that wasn't backed by scientific proof, but he'd thought enough of the book to lend it to her, so there must be some belief under his scepticism.

Not that he looked much like an academic this morning. He hadn't bothered to shave and wore a stained T-shirt and shorts that were frayed at the hem and faded to the color of putty. She supposed some women might consider him handsome, but she wasn't one of them. To her, he was just Adam. The one friend she could depend on. And one whose opinion she valued. "So what did you think of Passionata's theory that women hold the true power in any relationship?"

"You mean all that stuff about using sex to literally bring a man to his knees?" He snorted. "I've known guys like that—ones who usually think with their dicks and end up letting some woman lead them around by the balls. But I think they're the exception, not the rule." He refilled his coffee cup. "Take me, for instance. I like sex as well as the next guy, but it's not the be-all and end-all of my existence. Most of the time, it's not even in the top three of things on my agenda."

"You could get kicked out of the Real Man Club for saying that." She reached for a bagel and a jar of jam. "So you're saying you'd be immune to a woman like Passionata—an accomplished seductress?"

"You can only seduce someone who secretly wants to be seduced. I've got better things to do with my time."

Maybe so, but despite his belief otherwise, Nicole suspected Adam had his statistics backward and he was the exception to Passionata's rule. He was a man absorbed by his work—both teaching and his work-related hobby of hunting for artifacts. Everything else—personal grooming, eating and relationships—took a back seat to these passions.

But other men—men like Kenneth—certainly did seem to base much of their decisions in life on sex: how to get it; who to get it from; how to keep it; how to get more of it. Hadn't that been the reason Kenneth was sleeping with both her and the topless dancer from Pocono?

"So what's your interest in Passionata?" she asked.

"What's the first thing you think of when I say the word pirates?"

"Johnny Depp and Orlando Bloom?"

He rolled his eyes. "*Real* pirates, not movie pirates."

She shrugged. "I don't know. Treasure, I guess."

"Exactly." He wiped his hands on a paper napkin. "Last summer, after I found Passionata's autobiography, I started researching. I read everything I could get my hands on about her and her island headquarters. Have you got to the part in the book where she's captured?"

Nicole shook her head. "I fell asleep about a third of the way through." Not because the book didn't hold her interest, but because a day of sailing could wear a person out.

"I don't think I'll spoil it for you if I tell you she and her crew were trying to board a British merchant vessel when her ship—the *Eve*—ran onto the rocks and sank. The survivors of the wreck, including Passionata, were picked up by a second British Navy vessel. I've been searching through old nautical charts, seaman's diaries, oceanographic surveys and the like, and I think I've located the wreck."

"And the treasure." It all fit together now. Not only did Adam have a passion for history, he was a fiend for locating real-life artifacts related to the subjects he taught. He had spent previous summers volunteering with an archeological crew in Mexico, hunting for mastodon bones in the Black Hills and restoring Native American middens in Utah. So far most of his finds had done more to enhance his career than his bank account, but maybe that was about to change. "That's why you asked me to bring my diving gear," she said.

He nodded. "We won't have the time—or the money—to raise the ship and its contents. But I'm hoping we can locate enough items to interest backers who could fund a full-scale expedition next summer."

"What would something like that be worth?"

"Historically, it's virtually priceless. Shipwrecks of that antiquity are amazingly rare, and the kinds of artifacts I'd expect to find—weaponry, cutlery, gold and silver coins—would fetch a small fortune from collectors and museums. Easily in the millions. Possibly billions."

Her eyes widened. Adam laughed. "I'll give you a share if you help me."

"Since I'm unemployed at the moment, I can't say the money won't come in handy."

"You won't have any problem finding another job. Nurses are always in demand."

"True." She brushed crumbs from her shirt. "But this time I think I'll try a hospital. No more private clinics for me."

"You don't have to think about it now. Enjoy the summer. If we find the treasure, it'll be well worth your time. If not, at least you'll come home with a good story and a tan."

She was hoping for more than a story and a tan. In between studying Passionata's teachings and learning how to assert her female power, it might be fun to search for treasure. After all, if an ordinary woman could be powerful, then a *rich* woman might well be a superpower. "How long before we reach the island?" she asked.

"We'll stop off in Jamaica this afternoon for supplies, spend a couple days there taking in the sights, then sail for Passionata's Island. If the weather holds, we'll be there by the end of the week."

2

By THE TIME ADAM GUIDED the yacht into the harbor at Passionata's Island, Nicole was ready to dive off and swim to shore. The
promised couple of days in Jamaica had stretched to a week
after Adam ran into friends. For the next seven days he had
dragged Nicole from one beach party to barbecue to reggae
concert to the next. It had all been fun, but with each passing day
Nicole had grown more anxious to reach the island. She was
ready for solitude, adventure—and the chance to discover more
about the mysterious lady pirate who had also been duped by a
lying man yet had gotten her revenge in a big way.

Confessions of a Pirate Queen was still tucked under the
pillow in her bunk. Thanks to Adam's crammed social schedule,
she hadn't had the chance to read further in the book. One more
reason she looked forward to reaching the island and being *alone*.

Except, of course, for Adam. But she knew once he began the
work of looking for the wreck, he'd be completely preoccupied.
She'd have to remind him to eat, and only the fact that after sunset
it was too dark to dive would force him to sleep. No wonder he
was still single. No woman would put up with that kind of neglect
for months at a time.

"What do you think?" he asked as he wound down the anchor.
He'd snugged the yacht into a narrow lagoon shaded by tall
coconut palms. Waves broke against a spit of beige sand. In the

clear water she could see small fish and crabs. A stiff breeze rattled the palm fronds and softened the heat of the brilliant sun.

"It looks…like paradise." She turned to him, grinning. "Can we go ashore now?"

"Why not?" He unrolled a flexible aluminum ladder over the side of the boat and secured it, then swung onto it. Nicole scrambled down after him.

"The island is known for the coral reef offshore and the colorful fish," Adam said as he piloted the dinghy toward shore. "If it wasn't so remote, it would probably be really popular with divers."

"I like the idea of us having it to ourselves." She looked down into the crystal-clear water. It was like looking through a window to the ocean floor. "Are there any dangerous sea creatures I should be aware of?"

"The rays can hurt if they get you with their tails, so steer clear of them," he said. "And of course, there are sharks."

"Sharks?" She shuddered and glanced around her.

"They rarely come this close to shore. Just keep an eye out and you'll be fine." The dinghy scraped against the bottom and Adam jumped out to drag it onto the beach.

"You do realize if either of us is seriously injured, we're on our own out here," she said, the realization of what they could be getting into making her uneasy. The *idea* of an isolated paradise where one could say or do anything, unrestricted by rules or the opinions of others, was a tempting fantasy. But the reality of being completely on one's own was more daunting.

"We have a first-aid kit and you're a nurse," Adam said. "Anything you can't handle, we'll radio for help. But I don't plan on getting hurt."

She could have pointed out that no one *planned* on getting hurt, but what was the use? She could see Adam's mind was already on the treasure hunt ahead. In fact, he had plunged into the thick growth at the edge of the trees, onto a narrow path that led through a jungle of palms and other trees she couldn't identify.

"Where are you going?" she asked, running to catch up.

"Passionata's headquarters were in a stone tower near the center of the island," he said. "I want to see if I can find it."

Away from the open beach, the island was a different world. Tree trunks crowded the narrow path and blotted out the sun. The ground beneath was spongy with leaf mold, silencing their steps. The dense undergrowth prevented Nicole from seeing more than a few feet in front of her and on either side, but she could hear many unseen things: strange birds calling in the canopy overhead, small creatures scuttling on the jungle floor, tree branches scraping together, palm fronds rattling like rusty chains.

"It must have looked just like this when Passionata was here," she said softly.

"Hmmph." Adam grunted as he shoved a tangle of vines out of his way. "Remind me next time we come exploring to bring a machete."

"Do you have any idea where we're going?" she asked, looking around. She could barely make out the path they'd already traveled. "We're not going to get lost, are we?"

"The island is barely a mile wide. We won't get lost."

As if to prove his words, they suddenly emerged into a clearing. Nicole blinked in the bright sunlight and stared at a tumble of volcanic boulders in front of them. From this chaos of razor-sharp rock rose a fat stone tower, three stories high, pocked with narrow windows, the gray stone streaked liberally with white bird droppings.

In fact, there were birds everywhere—gulls wheeling and screaming overhead, perching on the rocks, strutting in the sand. The sound—and the smell—were almost overwhelming. She put her hands over her ears. "I don't think we're going to do much exploring here," she said, raising her voice to be heard over the din.

"Let's see what's on the other side." He led the way across the rocky clearing, birds fluttering out of their way at the last minute. Nicole shielded her head with her hands, just in case any offerings dropped from the sky.

The jungle growth on the other side of the tower was not as dense. Adam stopped to examine the ends of cut vines beside the path. "This looks fresh," he said.

"You mean, someone besides us is here?" she asked.

He didn't answer, but plunged ahead. Nicole stepped over fallen coconuts and sagging branches, hurrying to keep up with Adam's long strides.

She was so intent on watching her step on the uneven path she didn't realize he'd stopped until she collided with the solid wall of his back. "Ooooph," she grunted, pushing herself off of him. "What is it?"

He held out a hand and pointed. "Looks like we have company."

She leaned around him and stared. Some twenty yards away from them stood a palm-frond-covered shelter. Beneath it, slightly bent over something she couldn't see, his back to them, was a man.

A man with a muscular bronze back and shoulders, long legs and a nicely shaped and very naked backside. The whole man was naked, a fact Nicole's mind deduced in a microsecond, all while taking inventory of his delectable assets. Was this a descendant of one of Passionata's conquests? Or a modern-day Robinson Crusoe living alone on the island?

"Who the hell are you?" Adam demanded.

The naked man whirled to face them, clearly startled, then straightened himself to his full height. When he spoke, his voice was distinctly British and very proper. "I might ask you the same question."

IAN HAD SET HIMSELF a simple task for that morning—washing his clothes. At some point yesterday the magic potion the Jamaican woman had sold him had shattered in his luggage, leaving everything smelling like fermenting fruit—sweet and slightly intoxicating. When he'd first discovered the accident that morning, he'd laughed out loud. If the mysterious woman the old lady swore he'd meet ever did show up, he'd be on his own. Which was how he preferred things.

But, purely in the interest of scientific discovery, he sucked some of the liquid out of a sodden shirt, to see if it really would give him a hard-on that wouldn't quit.

It had not.

Doing laundry on a deserted island was not as simple as he'd expected, however. He had to collect rainwater from the cistern beside the tower, heat it over a fire, then scrub the clothes over rocks. Determined to repeat the task as seldom as possible, and not having seen another soul in the week he'd been on the island, he decided to wash everything at once and get it over with. In fact, he'd save wear and tear on his clothes in general if he went around naked most of the time. He liked the feel of the sun on his entire body. All part of getting in touch with his primitive side.

Only, now he was feeling at a decided disadvantage, facing this hulking man who'd emerged from the jungle. The big blond advanced toward him now, looking none too friendly. "I was told this island was uninhabited," the man said with an American accent.

"It is," Ian said. "I'm only visiting."

The blond glanced around at the shelter. Ian had spent the better part of three days erecting it, after he'd discovered living in the tower would be impossible. He was pleased with how it had turned out, proud to discover that, despite his academic background, he could work with his hands. "Looks pretty settled to me," the blond said.

"I'm staying the summer." Ian spotted the machete hanging by the door and moved toward it. Just in case.

"So are we," the man said.

We? Ian looked beyond the man and stared at the woman who was walking toward them. A tall, curvy brunette in a very small bikini. His physical response to this vision straight out of his most erotic fantasies was immediate and emphatic. He snatched a wet towel from the makeshift clothesline he'd hung at the back of the shelter and wrapped it around his waist. Unfortunately, this only served to emphasize his arousal, which tented out the towel like a pole.

The woman's cheeks were flushed, and she appeared to be holding back laughter. So much for him making a great first impression.

"I'm Nicole and this is my friend Adam," she said, offering her hand. "Don't pay any attention to him. He's an academic and doesn't know how to behave in public."

"Ian Marshall." He shook her hand, spirits plummeting further at her remark about academics. Not that the blond looked like much of an intellectual. More like a sea captain. Or one of the pirates the island was said to have once harbored.

"We've come to relax and do some diving," Nicole continued, ignoring the frown from her companion. "I hear the reefs here are spectacular. Have you seen them?"

He relaxed a little. "Yes. There are a number of rare species of fish here. Definitely worth seeing." One of his duties this summer was to photograph the fish and other native flora and fauna. Though he wasn't crazy about diving alone—it went against every safety rule in the book—once he'd decided on a solo trip he didn't have much choice. Fortunately, much of his work could be done snorkeling. When he did have to dive, he was extra careful with his equipment, and only allowed himself to stay down very limited amounts of time. It wasn't an ideal situation, but he thought he could make it work. He'd already used up rolls of film and a big chunk of the memory of his digital camera.

"So what are you, some kind of hermit?" Adam was still looking around the shelter, like a detective collecting evidence.

"I'm here doing research," Ian said.

"What kind of research?"

"Adam, don't be rude." Nicole put a hand on her companion's arm and smiled at Ian. A smile that made him a little dizzy. "I'm sure we'll be seeing more of you," she said. "But we'd better get back to our ship. We didn't mean to disturb you." Her gaze flickered over the towel, and laughter danced in her eyes. Then she turned and led Adam back across the rocks and into the jungle.

When he was sure they were gone, Ian sagged onto the wooden crate that doubled as a chair. So much for thinking he'd be spending the summer alone. Not that he was complaining about the woman. The thought of three months in a tropical paradise with her made him grateful Danielle what's-her-name had dumped him.

Was Nicole the woman the Jamaican had predicted—the one whose goal would be to wear him out? The idea was intriguing.

Of course, there was the matter of her disgruntled boyfriend to deal with. Yes, definitely a problem. Then again, Nicole might grow weary of her academic pirate's ill temper. Or decide she preferred dark, scholarly Englishmen.

And it might snow here tomorrow, too.

With a groan, he stood and attacked the washing with renewed vigor. But he kept the towel around his waist, just in case. It figured the only beautiful woman to show up on this deserted island was already attached to someone. So much for the Jamaican woman's prediction that he'd meet a great seductress.

Nicole had been friendly, but there was nothing overtly seductive about her, beyond the gorgeous figure, great hair and beautiful smile that would have attracted the attention of any man.

He finished the laundry and hung it to dry beneath the shelter, out of the reach of the birds, then looked around for something else to do. He could take his notebook and cameras and finish cataloging the plant life in the north lagoon, but he'd learned to avoid that sort of work in the hottest part of the day. His second day here he'd almost succumbed to sunstroke in the intense heat and humidity.

Better to take it easy for a couple of hours. Maybe catch up on his reading. He turned to the crate of books he'd brought along with him—a cookbook, a first-aid guide and half a dozen tomes on the ecology of the Caribbean, the subject of his doctoral thesis. But discussions of the life cycle of coral or poisonous plants of the South Seas held no appeal to him this afternoon, distracted as he was by memories of Nicole and Adam.

He spied a paperback among the books and drew it out. *Confessions of a Pirate Queen* was written across the front in bold red print, above a painting of a scantily clad woman on the gallows. He grinned. His buddy, Bryan Peachtree, had given him the book when he'd learned of Ian's plans for the summer. "If you're going to Passionata's Island, you should read this," he'd said with a wink. "I think you'll enjoy it."

No doubt some lurid soft-porn epic, Ian thought, settling into his hammock beneath a nearby pair of palms and opening the book. Bryan's idea of a joke. But since his encounter with Nicole had already put sex on his brain, why not?

BACK AT THE SHIP, Nicole prepared lunch while Adam checked his diving gear. "Why were you so rude to Ian?" she asked. "Now he's going to think we're ugly Americans."

"Judging by his reaction to you, I doubt *ugly* is the first word he thinks of." He spat into his snorkeling mask and rubbed the saliva around with his fingers.

"I'm not talking about me, I'm talking about you." She slapped cheese slices onto bread and began slicing an avocado. They'd be out of fresh produce before long—except coconuts, of course. And maybe she could find banana trees somewhere on the island. "Why were you so hostile to him?" she asked.

Adam set the snorkeling mask aside. "I guess I was looking forward to having the island to ourselves," he said. "How do we know he's not another treasure hunter, out to beat us to the find?"

"Isn't that the way these things work—finders keepers?" She handed him a sandwich, then took hers and sat across from him. "Who owns this island?"

"The British government. They've talked about building an airstrip here for years, but nothing's come of it."

"That treasure's been down there for three hundred years. Are you sure no one's recovered it before now?"

He nodded. "Pretty sure. It's hard to keep a find like that secret."

"Then there's no reason to believe Ian's after it, or that he even knows about it."

"Yeah, I guess you're right. I'll try to be nicer to him next time we meet."

"We should invite him to dinner," Nicole said. "I'll bet he's lonely."

Adam laughed. "Did you see the look on his face when he saw you? Pretty impressive boner you caused."

She stuck her tongue out at Adam, but she couldn't pretend she wasn't a little bit flattered. Seeing Ian's reaction to her had given her an inkling of the power Passionata was talking about. And Ian was a very good-looking man. Someone who could make her time on the island that much more interesting.

"What are you going to do this afternoon?" she asked Adam, changing the subject.

"I'm going to do some snorkeling, try to pin down the most likely location of the wreck. I'll take the Zodiac out. Do you want to come with me?"

She shook her head. "No. I think I'll stay here on the yacht and read. I came to relax, after all."

"Okay. But tomorrow I want us to go diving."

"We can do that. Tomorrow."

After lunch he inflated the Zodiac, fired up the motor and took off across the lagoon. Nicole brought her book out onto the deck and pulled a chaise into a shaded spot under the canopy. At last she could continue Passionata's adventures, and learn more about her approach to male/female relationships.

The story has been told of how I and my crew, like the Sirens of legend, would lure sailors to the rocks and their undoing. When these lonely men, long at sea, would spy our fair forms reclining near the sea, most seductively arrayed and beckoning, they seldom resisted long. Even after word of the hazard we posed passed among the sailing crews, they were loathe to avoid us. Indeed, it is said many sought us out, though their defeat was inevitable.

What has not been told—until now—is what happened to those men who survived the wreck and battle. The fate of those who became our prisoners. The bravest and best of these became our slaves and courtesans. They served at our pleasure, as women have been made to do for centuries. But this time the women were in charge, and the men were at our mercy.

They were wont to resist at first, but soon learned the futility of this. And more than a few discovered a taste for subservience. For though they had been raised to always be in charge—in control—they discovered the erotic nature of surrender.

The chapter ended, and, breath quickening, Nicole turned the page and found the narrative interrupted by a note from the editor.

Though *Confessions of a Pirate Queen* first appeared as a serial printed in the *London Times* in 1715, the following portion of the original manuscript was deemed too obscene for public consumption, and was unknown for more than two centuries, until an original of the entire document was discovered in the *London Times*'s archives in 1993.

Here, Passionata's narrative resumed:

When a woman is in control of a relationship, everything changes. No longer is she at the mercy of a man's wishes and desires, subjugating her own wants and needs to his timetable. Now he must serve *her* desires. And, as the men who served the women of Passionata's Island soon discovered, a woman in charge of her own sexual destiny discovers a true flowering of desire, and a capacity for sexual pleasure heretofore unknown.

It is an arrangement of benefit to both man and woman—as illustrated by the story of William D., a sailor who came to Passionata's Island in the summer of 1707.

"We have the prisoners ready to present to you, madame." My lieutenant, a dusky woman who had taken the name of Determinata, appeared in the doorway of my tower headquarters the morning after our most recent conquest of a British merchant vessel. The vessel had been carrying a cargo of gold bullion, silver coins and exotic spices, and we had spent a good part of the night securing the wreckage. Today the divers would begin retrieving the spoils from the hold and adding them to our stores.

"How many today?" I asked. It had been a large ship, but the battle had been fierce. The sharks would have feasted well last night.

"Seven. One is only a boy, but the others…" Determinata smiled. "There are some very fine specimens here."

"Then I must see them."

I followed her down the stone staircase and out into the plaza in front of the tower. It was a fine day, hot and clear. The men stood bare-chested, hands bound behind their backs.

One caught my eye. He was lean and tall, with the dark hair and fair skin of a continental. I stopped before him and he looked me in the eye, defiant. He was well muscled, with a fine dusting of black hair across his chest, narrow hips and strong legs. "What is your name?" I asked.

I could read in his eyes that he thought of not answering. But I kept my gaze on him, unflinching, and at last he said, "William."

His accent was British and upper class. Perhaps the son of the ship owner, or a nobleman or tradesman who had purchased passage. Looking into his eyes, at the spirit there, I felt the heat build inside me. "William, you will come with me," I said, and turned to walk back to my tower.

"Why should I come with you?" he asked, his tone haughty.

I didn't turn around. I liked the question, but there was no hesitation in my answer. "Because if you don't, one of my lieutenants will shoot you, and that would be a waste of good flesh."

I anticipated he might need more persuading, but after a moment's hesitation, he fell into step behind me. I kept my back to him, hoping he wouldn't be foolish enough to try to overpower me or to run away. My guards would be watching him and they would shoot to kill.

But he made no such attempt and soon we were alone in my tower room. I bade him sit, and had one of my other servants, Marcus, bring him water and bread. William eyed the man with distaste. "Is this what you intend for me?" he asked. "To make me your slave?"

"The choice is yours," I said, but explained no further. He would choose his own role here—slave or courtesan. I wanted him for my bed, but if he was unwilling, I would not force him. Men overpower reluctant women with rape. I preferred to use my sexual prowess to teach men the advantages of accepting my superiority and command.

While he ate, I made myself comfortable, divesting myself of my outer garments, revealing the sheer silk undersheath. I unbanded and combed out my long hair, all the while acting as if he was no longer in the room. I loosened the straps of my gown and rubbed scented lotion into my shoulders and across the top of my breasts, caressing myself, watching in the mirror as he watched me.

And he was indeed watching me, the remainder of his meal forgotten. One glance showed me the tightness at the front of his trousers. Yes, this one would make a good courtesan.

"Do you like what you see?" I asked him.

The question startled him. He snapped his gaze away. "Who would like being a prisoner?"

"In the world beyond this island, every woman is a

prisoner—of her father or her husband or of the rules society has laid out for her. Most have learned to live with it."

"But you did not," he said.

"I did not. I have made my own kingdom, with my own rules."

"And now the men are prisoners," he said, frowning.

I nodded. "But it is not such an unpleasant existence for them, I tell you."

He made a noise like a growl. I ignored him and sat on a high stool across from him. The light from the window was at my back, making my gown almost transparent. I wanted him to know what awaited him if he was willing.

I could feel his eyes burning into me, and imagined that same heat coursing through his body, into mine. "Are you trying to seduce me?" he asked after a moment.

I laughed. "Of course." I leaned toward him, my breasts straining against the front of my gown. "Do you want to be seduced?"

He looked at my breasts, then back into my eyes. "What happens if I say yes?"

"That is part of the excitement, isn't it?" I leaned closer still, and lowered my voice to just above a whisper. "But I promise, I have had no complaints yet."

His eyes locked to mine, and tension radiated from him, vibrating the air. "What do I have to do?" he asked, his voice roughened by desire.

I smiled, and straightened to my full height, looking down on him. "That is the best part," I said. "You will do whatever I tell you."

3

NICOLE CLOSED THE BOOK and took a deep breath. Whew! Her skin felt too tight for her body, and there was a persistent throbbing between her legs. What Passionata had done was amazing. So empowering. And erotic.

Looking back, Nicole could see that in every relationship in her life, she had allowed the man to take charge. Even in these liberated times, it was how society was designed to operate. The man asked for a date. The man made the first move sexually, and in Nicole's case, almost every move afterward.

How much different would it have been if she had taken charge, if she had approached each sexual encounter with the focus on satisfying her own desires instead of placating her partner? Certainly such an approach would have left her with fewer regrets about Kenneth…and maybe a few more orgasms.

Okay, she definitely needed to cool down a little. She decided to go for a walk to clear her head and found herself heading toward Ian's camp on the opposite side of the island. Maybe without Adam's bristling presence, she could get to know their fellow islander better, and issue that invitation to dinner.

She fought her way through the jungle, and hurried across the clearing, past the tower and its raucous avian residents. A little out of breath, she stopped in the trees looking out onto Ian's camp, reluctant to barge in on him in case he was naked again.

Not that she hadn't enjoyed seeing him in the altogether, but she didn't want to embarrass him further.

The shelter appeared empty except for the shirts and pants that hung from the line there, doing a desultory dance in the erratic breeze. She turned her attention to the rest of the camp: the neat fire ring encircled by log seats, boxes and barrels providing further seating around the area, dive equipment waiting in a neat pile beside a table and bench built of scrap lumber. But no sign of Ian. .

Disappointed, she started to turn away, then a movement in the shade of a coconut palm on the edge of the camp caught her attention. As she peered closer, she recognized a hammock. Someone was in it, and she slipped around through the trees until she could get a better view.

Ian looked as good lying down as he had standing, legs outstretched, sun dappled over his lean chest and torso. The towel that had been wrapped around him had fallen to the side and the hammock was swaying gently back and forth, driven by the rhythm of the hand which stroked his erect penis.

Her breath caught as the reality of what he was doing registered. She stared, fascinated, at the strong brown fingers wrapped around his thick erection. His chin was on his chest, his mouth slightly open, his eyes closed, his expression one of intense concentration.

She heard his breathing, harsh and rapid, and found herself panting in response. Her nipples were hard buds pressed against the cups of her bikini top and she squeezed her thighs against the throbbing tension between her legs.

He groaned, and his hand moved faster. Light glinted on a drop of moisture at the tip of his penis. Nicole covered her breasts with her hands and bit her lip to keep from moaning. As he continued to pump his hand, she began to massage her aching breasts, squeezing the nipples, twirling them between her thumb and forefinger, the tension and wetness building between her legs.

She kept her eyes open, focused on Ian's face, on the shock of dark hair falling across his forehead, the lines of tension around his eyes and mouth, and the fierceness of his expression. Her rapid breathing matched his, and every muscle strained with his.

His hand began to move faster, and the hammock rocked more violently. Nicole swayed also, her legs quivering. Sweat ran down her back and gathered at the top of her buttocks. The air was humid and thick with the scent of her musk.

With a loud cry, he came, his body arching in the hammock, the seminal fluid painting his torso in glistening stripes. Nicole leaned against the trunk of a palm tree and closed her eyes, slipping one hand beneath the waistband of her bikini bottoms as she did so.

Using her own moisture as a lubricant, she fingered her clit, rolling it back and forth beneath her thumb, biting the finger of her other hand to stifle her moans. She was only dimly aware of the rough bark abrading her bare back, of the screaming of gulls overhead or the oppressive heat of the afternoon sun. Her legs began to tremble violently and she moved her hand faster, breathing rapidly.

She came hard, slamming back into the tree trunk, her whole body shuddering, one sharp cry escaping her lips. She smiled, amazed at what she'd just done—and how wonderful and illicit and…decadent…it had felt.

She turned her head to look toward the hammock again and was alarmed to see Ian sitting up now. He held the towel in one hand and was frowning toward the jungle where she'd hidden herself. He must have heard her cry. Had he seen her?

Not bothering to wait for an answer, she took off, sprinting down the narrow path, not stopping until she reached the yacht, where she lay for a long time in the chaise on the deck, marveling at what had happened.

IAN SPENT THE NEXT morning snorkeling and photographing marine life around the coral reef. He kept an eye out for Adam and Nicole. He'd just as soon avoid the one—but looked forward to the chance to talk to the other. He hadn't been able to stop thinking about her, perhaps influenced by the chunk of *Confessions of a Pirate Queen* he'd read after they'd left him yesterday afternoon. The erotic tale, combined with his erotic fantasies of Nicole, had resulted in him jacking off in the hammock. When he was done he had the eerie sensation he was being watched, and had thought he heard someone—or something—in the jungle nearby. But by the time he'd recovered enough to investigate, there was no one there.

Had Adam been watching him? Or Nicole?

The idea that his voyeur had been the curvy brunette made him hard all over again. Was it that book, or this place, or merely the fact that he'd never spent so much time alone before, that had him so horny? Or was his increased interest in sex one more aspect of his quest to prove himself a real man?

He forced himself to focus on his work, aiming his camera at a red-and-white sea anemone clinging to the coral along the outer edge of the reef. As he snapped the shutter, he spotted the bright yellow-and-black form of a rock beauty angelfish swimming away from the coral and followed it with his lens.

The fish darted away, and his viewfinder was suddenly filled with a pair of long, slender legs. A woman's very sexy legs. He followed them up and found himself looking at Nicole. She was wearing diving tanks, a short wetsuit, flippers and a mask. She smiled and waved, and signaled for him to meet her up top.

They broke through the surface together. She pushed her mask down to dangle around her neck and he did likewise. Water streamed from her hair, and droplets glistened on the tops of her breasts showing above her partially unzipped wetsuit top.

Ian imagined what it would be like to lick the drops off her, one by one.

"I'm sorry if I scared off that fish you were photographing," she said, pulling him from his fantasy. "But I wanted to talk to you."

He started to make some comment about there being plenty of fish in the sea and realized how lame that would sound. Instead he focused on stowing his camera and trying to appear nonchalant. "What did you want to talk to me about?"

"I wanted to invite you to have dinner with us soon. Tonight, if you like."

Even without the added pleasure of spending more time with her, the prospect of eating something besides his own cooking was reason enough to accept the invitation. "I'd like that," he said. "Thanks."

They treaded water side by side, bobbing in the waves that broke steadily over the reef. The island was a line of trees a quarter mile distant. He could see his Zodiac, a splash of orange where he'd anchored it at the other end of the reef. Where had Nicole come from? Had she swum from shore or did she have a boat somewhere?

"How long have you been on the island?" she asked.

"Eight days." He shook his head. "Though if I didn't mark off the days on the calendar it would be easy to lose track." He looked around, at the sun sparkling on the water and the seabirds circling overhead. "Time doesn't mean much out here, when there's no schedule to keep."

"It sounds heavenly." She glanced at him. "I worked at a doctor's office until recently. Sometimes I felt as if my whole life was divided into fifteen-minute increments."

"You don't have to worry about that out here. It's strange, but I can spend all day working on a project and never realize hours have gone by until it starts to get dark. When I was building that shelter I worked on into the night. It didn't matter, because I knew I could sleep as long as I wanted the next day." He shrugged. "Very different from the kind of life I usually lead." He wondered if he was talking too much. He wasn't normally garrulous, but after a week of silence it was as if he had all these words dammed up inside of him that had to be let out.

"What kind of life is that?" she asked, apparently not minding that he'd rambled on so. "What do you do?"

He hesitated. Here he'd just painted this picture of himself as a rugged adventurer, building his own shelter, living on the island alone. If he admitted he was a doctoral student, he'd ruin the image. And he couldn't forget the dig she'd made yesterday about her friend, Adam, being an academic who didn't know how to behave. "I'm a writer," he said. It wasn't exactly untrue. He was here working on his dissertation, among other things.

"How exciting! What do you write? Adventure stories? Suspense?"

Better not let this get out of hand. "My focus right now is on writing about the environment." *Did that sound too dull?* "But I'm playing with the idea of writing something about the history of the island," he added. "Pirates and everything." *Where the hell had that come from?*

"I'm reading a book right now about a female pirate who had her headquarters here," she said.

"Confessions of a Pirate Queen?"

She laughed. "Yes. You know it?"

"I'm familiar with it." Yesterday he'd only read as far as the pirate's seduction of William D. Lying in his hammock, so close to the very spot where the activities in the book had supposedly taken place, it had been easy to imagine himself as the captured sailor and Nicole as the woman taunting him and commanding his attention.

"She lived in that tower near your camp—the one with all the birds," Nicole said.

"When I first arrived here, I planned to use the tower as my headquarters," he said. "That idea didn't last long once I saw—and smelled—all those birds." He wrinkled his nose at the memory. "There's a cistern there that I use for fresh water," he added. "It's covered and I rigged up a filter for the drain pipe."

"That's handy to know. You've really made yourself at home here, haven't you? I was impressed with what I saw of your camp."

"It still needs improvements." As if he built his own shelter every day of the week and had big plans for this place.

She moved closer. "But aren't you lonely, here all by yourself?"

Her voice was soft. Caressing. He had to restrain himself from reaching out and touching her. Her eyes looked into his, searching. For what? To ascertain if he was entirely sane? After all, who but a crazy person would voluntarily spend the summer alone on a deserted island?

"Originally my girlfriend was going to come with me," he said.

"Oh? Why didn't she?"

"She decided she'd rather spend the summer with her new boyfriend instead."

"Ouch!"

He shrugged. "The trip was already planned, so I decided to come out here on my own. I really don't mind my own company, most of the time."

A wave rolled over them, driving them apart, and he kicked his feet to move nearer to her once more. "So you and your boyfriend are here for the diving?" he asked.

"My boy—" She laughed and shook her head. "Adam is *not* my boyfriend. Just an old friend. Really."

Really. He felt considerably lighter at this news. Almost giddy. "That's great."

She smiled, as if at a private joke. "Yes, it is, isn't it?"

They were interrupted by the loud whine of a Zodiac approaching. Adam pulled the boat alongside them and idled the engine. "Hello, Marshall." He nodded. The greeting wasn't effusive, but at least today the man wasn't hostile.

"Hello," Ian said.

"Ian's coming to dinner with us tonight," Nicole said.

"That's good." Adam gave him a long look. "We should all get to know each other better." He turned to Nicole. "You ready to go?"

"I guess so." She paddled to the side of the Zodiac and Adam leaned over to help her in. Ian stayed back, enjoying the very nice view of her legs and backside as she climbed into the rubber craft.

"See you around seven," she called as Adam piloted the boat away.

Only five hours. He couldn't wait.

"WHAT WAS HE UP to out there?" Adam asked Nicole when Ian was out of sight.

"He was photographing fish and coral and stuff." She pulled off her mask and combed her hair back out of her face.

"Not hunting for shipwrecks?"

She scowled at him. "No, he wasn't hunting for shipwrecks."

Adam gunned the outboard motor and the prow of the Zodiac rose out of the water. Nicole gripped the handhold on the side of the boat and braced herself against each slap of the hull against the surface of the water. Normally, she found the speed exhilarating, but now she was annoyed that Adam was venting his feelings this way.

"Did he say what he was doing here?" Adam shouted over the roar of wind, water and the outboard motor.

"He mentioned something about wanting to write a history of

the island. He knew about *Confessions of a Pirate Queen*." The knowledge that he'd probably read the same erotic passages she'd enjoyed added heat to her attraction to him. Ian would be the perfect person to help her discover her sexual power.

Adam frowned toward the horizon. "If he does that he'll have half the amateur treasure hunters in the world descending on this place."

"Then, you'll have to find the shipwreck before he's published."

Adam slowed the boat as they neared the shore. Nicole gathered her hair in a knot at the back of her head and held it with one hand as she turned to look back at him. "Did you have any luck this afternoon?" she asked.

He shook his head. "I'm going to refigure my coordinates this evening. We have to be close—reports of the wreck mention the reef."

"I'm sure you'll find it. We have all summer."

"The sooner we find it, the more work we can do before we have to leave." His eyes met hers, his expression grave. "I want some impressive artifacts to show potential backers."

"You'll find them. You always do." She smiled. "Thanks for inviting me to come with you. This really is exactly what I needed."

"You're welcome. Besides, I needed the help. Not to mention you're a better cook than I am."

She turned to look over the prow once more. She could see the yacht now, nestled in the cove, much of the deck shaded by the awning Adam had erected that morning. "I think we might as well grill the last of our steaks tonight," she said. "They're not going to last much longer in this heat."

"You're just trying to impress Marshall," Adam said.

Her only answer to this taunt was a smile. She *was* trying to impress Ian. His dark intensity attracted her. His body wasn't bad, either.

She was intrigued, too, by Passionata's theories about male/female relationships. Like Nicole herself, Passionata had been betrayed by a man she'd loved. But instead of throwing a pity party, the pirate had exacted a more rewarding revenge—one that was financially profitable and, to judge by the portions of her autobiography Nicole had read so far—physically satisfying.

Nicole would leave the financial spoils up to Adam and his treasure hunt. But she was eager to test Passionata's approach to physical pleasure.

Here on this island, she was declaring her personal mutiny from all the rules about how a nice girl should act that had constrained her until now. Granted, going against years of teaching and habit wouldn't be easy. As daring as she'd felt yesterday afternoon watching Ian in his hammock, in the end she'd run away rather than risk being caught. Which proved she needed all the practice she could get. What better way to start her transformation than to commit her own modern-day act of piracy and seduce the handsome Englishman? They'd give a whole new meaning to the words *tropical paradise*.

4

IAN ARRIVED AT NICOLE and Adam's yacht as the sun painted the western sky in orange and pink. He wore clean khaki shorts and a cotton shirt—the most clothing he'd had on since arriving at the island, and even that looked like formal wear compared to Adam's faded swim trunks and tank top.

"Hello." Nicole greeted him from the open door of the cabin. She wore a strapless red dress made of some silky material that floated in the breeze, the full skirt swirling around the tops of her thighs. She held a bottle of wine in one hand, and a trio of glasses in the other. "Would you like some wine?"

"Sounds great." He held out the covered bowl that contained his own contribution to the meal. "I brought some mussels, poached in olive oil and wine. They're everywhere in the tidal flat on my side of the island."

"Sounds yummy." She carried the wine and glasses to a small round table on the deck and he followed. "I'll get some plates and forks and we'll have them for our appetizer." She handed the bottle to Adam. "Would you open this, please?"

Adam grabbed a corkscrew and attacked the bottle of wine. "The coals are almost ready for the steaks," he said. Waves of heat rose from the good-size grill on the other side of the deck.

"This is a beautiful yacht," Ian said, leaning against the rail. It was an older-model sailing yacht that had obviously been well maintained, the woodwork polished and the paint a crisp white.

"I inherited her from my uncle," Adam said. "He taught me to sail and knew I'd love her as much as he had. She has an eight-horsepower diesel engine and full cruising and racing sails."

Ian nodded. He knew little or nothing about sailing or engines and cared less. But he'd never admit it to Long John Silver here.

Nicole returned with the plates and forks and they sat down to wine and mussels. After her first mouthful, Nicole closed her eyes and moaned, a sound that sent Ian's blood racing south. "These are delicious," she said.

"Thanks. I'll show you where to find them, if you like."

"Is there much food on the island?" Adam asked, spearing a fat mussel with his fork. "Besides coconuts, mussels and fish?"

"Sure, there's all kinds of stuff—different herbs and fruits. Purslane, sea grapes, wild yams and carrots and, of course, bananas."

"And you've discovered all this in a week?" Nicole asked. "I'm impressed."

He nodded, deciding against elaborating. In his work cataloging the island's flora and fauna he'd naturally come across all the edible species.

"I took the Zodiac all around the island today and didn't see a ship," Adam said. "How did you get here?"

Had Adam been checking up on him, or was he merely making an observation? "I booked passage on a merchant vessel whose route took it near here."

"Weren't you worried something might happen and you'd need to leave and couldn't?" Nicole asked.

He had worried about this some. When Danielle had declined to accompany him, he'd even debated abandoning the idea of a solo trip. But he'd convinced himself that as long as he was careful, the risks were small, and worth the payoffs, which he hoped would include a better sense of his capabilities. He needed to challenge himself and test his limits. Risk was part of the test.

"I have a radio I can use to summon help," he said.

"Still, it's a big gamble," Adam said. "One slip with a machete and it could be all over. Not to mention diving alone is foolhardy."

Ian nodded. "It's a risk I was willing to take."

The last of the mussels eaten, Adam pushed away his empty plate. "We'd better put the steaks on," he said.

"They're in the galley." Nicole sat back and sipped the wine. "Ready when you are."

Ian hid a smile as he watched the realization hit Adam that Nicole had no intention of fetching the steaks for him. But the big man recovered quickly and retreated to the cabin.

"It's a beautiful evening, isn't it?" Nicole said when they were alone. She looked out over the rail at the sunset, which had faded to deep maroon and orange streaks across a silver sky. "I think I'm going to like it here." She glanced at him. "Is it like this every night?"

"Except when it rains, which it's done only once since I've been here, though I understand in July and August it sometimes rains every afternoon, briefly."

"We won't have to worry about fresh water, then," she said. "And I love those soft, tropical rains. There's something very…sensual about them, don't you think?" She traced her index finger up and down the stem of her wineglass, eyes locked to his, telegraphing a message that had nothing to do with rain.

Or maybe that was only his overheated brain imagining she was stroking something other than a wineglass.

Adam returned with the steaks and hijacked the conversation once more. "Nicole says you're a photographer," he said. "That you've been photographing the reef."

"Yes. I'm cataloging the sea life here."

"For a book?" He forked the slabs of meat onto the grill.

Ian shifted in his chair. "Maybe." Time to turn the tables and interrogate Adam for a while. "What's your interest here?" he asked. "There are a lot of places to dive."

Adam ignored the question. He refilled his glass and leaned against the rail. "Nicole said you know a lot about the history of the island."

"Some."

"I'm a history professor. Michigan State University. I'm interested in the nautical history of this area."

"You mean pirates."

Obviously Adam hadn't expected this. He studied Ian through narrowed eyes for a moment. "Why do you say that?"

"Pirates are about the only thing significant in Passionata's Island's history that I'm aware of. That and the curse."

"A curse?" Nicole leaned forward in her chair. "What curse?"

He had their attention now, and took his time finishing his wine and setting aside his glass before he proceeded. "Well, the story is that on the gallows, Passionata pronounced a curse on the island. She said no one would ever again be able to live here, that her treasure would be forever hidden and that only disaster would befall any who tried to recover it or reclaim the island."

Nicole's dark eyes clouded and she glanced at Adam. "I hadn't heard that."

"Fairy tales." Adam checked the steaks, then sat across from Ian once more. "History is full of things like that, mostly apocryphal."

Ian shrugged. "All I can tell you is that the treasure has apparently never been found—if the British government actually left any behind when they cleared the island in late 1714. In the 1820s, settlers from Jamaica tried to establish a colony here. They were wiped out by disease. The island itself was almost completely destroyed by a hurricane in 1850."

The skepticism left Adam's eyes, replaced by a definite interest. "Tell me more about this hurricane."

"I don't know much more," Ian said. "There was a major storm here around 1850 that completely submerged the island and destroyed most of the vegetation. From what I've read, it took more than a hundred years for the jungle to return to its present condition."

"But Passionata's tower survived," Nicole said.

"Yes," he said. "If you check out the construction of that thing, it's rooted deep in solid rock. The bottom walls are three feet thick. It's as close to indestructible as a man-made building can be."

"Steaks are ready," Adam announced and began forking them onto a plate.

Nicole brought out potatoes and they settled in to eat. Not having had fresh beef for more than a week, Ian's attention was riveted for the first ten minutes of the meal.

But gradually, his hunger sated, he became more aware of the woman across from him at the table. When he looked up, he found Nicole's gaze fixed on him. And judging by the mysterious smile that played about her mouth, she wasn't unhappy with what she saw.

As soon as dinner was over, Adam excused himself to go below. The abruptness of his departure surprised Ian. "What's his problem?" he asked Nicole as he helped her clean up.

"Don't mind him," she said. "When he fixes his mind on something, he's the typical absentminded professor. He forgets to eat or sleep or anything."

Ian glanced toward the door to the cabin. "What's on his mind right now?"

She shrugged and picked up a stack of plates. "Probably hurricanes or curses—no telling what you said that set him off." She grinned. "But at least you and I will be alone now."

He smiled back. "Let's leave the dishes for later," he said.

"Oh, I intend to. I'm going to leave them for Adam to do. After all, I did most of the cooking."

Carrying the assortment of glasses, he followed her to the galley. "How do you and Adam know each other?" he asked, mentally bracing himself for the news that they were former lovers.

"We were roommates for a while, in a house with a couple of other people." She filled the galley's tiny sink with dishes and glanced over her shoulder at him. "I guess we hit it off because he's one of the few men I've been around who treated me like one of the guys. I feel about him the same way I feel about my brother."

"He treats you like one of the guys? What—is he gay?"

She laughed. "Not at all. There's just no physical chemistry between us. And we don't want there to be."

"So…is there a man in your life? A romantic relationship?"

"There was." She turned to face him. "Until I found out that for most of the time he'd been seeing me, he was also sleeping with a topless dancer he met at some sleazy club. Probably others, as well."

Ian winced. "Guess we're in the same boat."

She raised her chin and studied him for a moment. He was silent, waiting, expectation electrifying the air. He was certain now that the sexual attraction he felt was not one-sided. Normally he would have made the first move to establish that, but with Nicole he was willing to wait. Waiting only served to heighten his excitement.

After a moment she walked out onto the deck. He followed, his eyes focused on the straight line of her spine, the soft curve of her hips, the gentle swaying of the silken fabric falling over her buttocks.

She stopped at the rail and stood looking out into the darkness. He could hear the slap of waves against the side of the yacht and the insistent, high-pitched peeps of tree frogs in the jungle behind them.

"What do you think of Passionata's theories?" she asked after a moment.

"Her theories?"

"Yes. Her belief that male/female relationships work out best if the woman is in charge."

"It was certainly an unusual idea for its time." He stood next to her, his back to the ocean, watching her. Though much of her face was in shadow, he could make out the soft curve of her cheek, the half smile on her lips. The breeze stirred tendrils of her dark hair and brought the smell of her perfume to him, exotic and floral. "It's still an unusual idea."

"But do you think it's a good one?"

"Why does anyone have to be in charge of a relationship?" he asked.

She faced him, moving closer, so that the skirt of her dress brushed against his legs, a teasing caress. "If you had been a man of that time," she said, "if you had been William D., would you have allowed her to seduce you?"

He had a sharp memory of the scenes in Passionata's book where she toyed with the captured sailor, and arousal lanced through him. But just because the idea of an act or situation turned him on didn't mean it was what he really wanted. "I don't think that's a question I can answer," he said. "I'm a man of today."

She turned away. "Oh, yes, the rugged individualist who comes to the island by himself, risk be damned," she said.

"Do you think I'm a crazy fool?"

She looked at him once more, eyes boring into him. "What if I said I intended to seduce you?" she asked. "Would you see it as a threat...or a fantasy?"

Maybe both. But his heart beat faster at her words. "What are you getting at?" he asked.

"Come with me." She took his hand and led him to the ladder at the side of the ship. "Let's go for a walk on the beach."

Maybe she wanted to get further away from Adam to do her seducing, he speculated, as he followed her down the ladder and onto the dinghy. When they reached the beach he kicked off his sandals and buried his toes in the cool sand. Protected by the reef and uninhabited for years, Passionata's Island offered a beach free of litter, broken glass and other man-made hazards.

Nicole took his hand and led him to a hammock strung between two palm trees. "Lie down," she commanded and pushed him back into the hammock.

He did as she asked, expecting her to lie beside him. But instead, she crawled on top of him, and straddled his stomach. Her thighs clenched him tightly, and he could feel the heat of her sex through the thin cotton of his shirt.

She planted her palms on his chest and stared down at him, her expression serious. "Yes or no?" she said. "Do you want to be seduced?"

If he said no, would she leave? And what would he have gained by this defense of his dignity? He thought of Passionata and William D., and the passages the long-ago London censors had labeled obscenity.

"Yes," he said. Then again. "Yes."

NICOLE STARED DOWN at Ian and recognized the anxiety that flickered through his eyes, though his body beneath her remained relaxed. Heat rushed through her—the heat of desire, and also a great sensation of power. This man was at her mercy, subject to her wishes and desires, and the knowledge made her feel stronger and more confident in herself than she remembered ever feeling. Was this what Passionata had felt, as well?

Her eyes locked to his, she reached up and grasped the top of her dress, then lowered the silky fabric over her breasts—slowly—revealing an inch of naked skin at a time, feeling the cool slide of silk over her flesh, watching as Ian's eyes darkened with desire, listening to the increased pace of his breathing.

Passionata had uncovered herself this way before the captured sailor, whose hands were bound behind his back. "You may touch me." Passionata had said. "But only with your mouth."

William had looked at her for a long moment before doing so, his physical desires warring with the resistence required by dignity and convention and all the things that held him back. But in the end he had pleased both himself and Passionata.

Nicole put her hands on Ian's chest. "You read Passionata's book," she said.

"Yes. I read the book." His voice was rough edged, his breathing ragged.

She bent forward, lowering her breasts toward his mouth. He turned his head, and she shuddered as his tongue swept across one nipple, then the other. Eyes shut tightly, she gave herself up to the sensations of velvet heat followed by the chilling breeze across her moist flesh. Her nipples drew up into tight beads, tender and aching.

He put his hand at her back, and urged her closer. When he began to suckle, pulling hard, then caressing with his tongue, she began to pant and rock against him. She could feel his erection pressed against her bottom, hot and very hard. She widened her legs, pressing her aching sex against his stomach, still rocking gently, almost believing she would make herself come from even this tenuous touch.

He arched against her, rubbing his erection against her bottom, his mouth still caressing and teasing her breasts. She felt herself losing control of the situation, something she didn't want. Not this early in the game.

She pulled back and took in a deep breath of the moist sea air. She looked out at the empty beach, remembering what had happened next in the book. Passionata had stopped at this point. She'd reached down and taken hold of William's penis, squeezing "until his eyes lost focus and his mouth went slack."

Then she had stepped back, told him he wasn't hard enough for her yet, they would continue later. She had sent the poor man away then, his hands tied so that he couldn't relieve his own torment.

In that moment, Nicole believed Passionata had not been seeing William, but the pirate who had betrayed her. She was taking her revenge on him, and on all men by making sure they understood that on her island, she called the shots.

Nicole looked at Ian, who stared up at her, his eyes wary, waiting. Was he thinking of what had happened in the book as well? He wasn't tied up or a prisoner, but she still held the power to refuse him relief.

She had no intention of doing so. And she would be denying herself, as well. Smiling, she slid down his body, pausing to arch against his erection, gasping as it brushed against her sensitive core.

She unfastened the buttons on his shirt while he massaged the silk of her dress over her hips. She had a sense that he was fighting the instinct to pull her close and demand they get on with this.

She pushed the shirt back to bare his chest, then began to kiss him, letting her lips discover his taste and texture, the roughness of the coarse brown hair on his chest, the hard bud of his erect nipples, the defined ridge of each rib. He smelled of salt and castile soap and the wine they'd had for dinner. And sex. He smelled of desire and passion, of wantonness and a freedom she'd never allowed herself before now.

She trailed her tongue along the line of hair that disappeared beneath the waistband of his shorts. His erection bulged the fly, and she cradled him for a moment, savoring the feel. "You seem plenty hard enough for me," she said, smiling.

"Get these shorts off and I'll show you hard," he said, arching once more.

But again she resisted the urge to rush. Taking her time was proving all too delicious. Based on her past experiences, only when she was in charge would she have the chance to enjoy such leisurely foreplay.

She toyed with the button at the top of the shorts, and slipped her hands beneath the waistband, where her fingers brushed against the head of his penis. He jerked against her and she felt a corresponding twitch deep inside.

Then she unfastened the button and stroked one finger along the zipper, pressing the ridges of the zipper into his swollen flesh, eliciting a long sigh.

When at last she lowered the zipper and peeled back his underwear, she found him stiff and heavy. The thought of having him soon inside her made her squirm with pleasure.

But not yet. She wanted to play this hand as long as she dared, to take them both to the very brink before satisfying their desire. Knowing she had the power to do so was as arousing as the sight of him naked before her.

She helped him out of his shorts, then stood beside the hammock and stripped off her dress and panties, her back to him, as if he did not concern her at all. But she was aware of his gaze on her, burning into her. The heat of that stare melted into her with an intensity even the night breeze couldn't cool.

She climbed into the hammock once more. It was wide, with oak bars at either end to hold it open and a blanket spread across the ropes to add comfort. There was room for them to lie side by side, but she chose to straddle him once more. To imprison him between her thighs and be the one to dictate each move.

"What now?" he asked, stroking the sides of her torso down to her hips.

She smiled. "You'll have to wait and find out."

She started to slide toward his knees, but his hand on her arm stopped her. "This probably isn't the best time to bring this up, but do you have any condoms?"

She laughed. "No, I didn't sail to a deserted island with boxes of condoms. How about you?"

He shook his head, worry lines creasing his forehead. She thought he muttered a particularly foul curse, but she was laughing too much to hear him clearly.

"What's so funny?" he asked.

She shook her head. "You don't have to worry about anything. I'm on the pill, and the one thing Dr. Jerk was good about was protection. After I found out about his other bed partners, I had myself tested, but everything's fine. Unless…" The thought stole all her laughter. "You haven't got any problems I should know about?"

He shook his head. "No. I'm healthy, I promise."

"Then we don't have anything to worry about." She smiled and directed her attention to his erection once more. "Now, where were we?"

"You were telling me I had to wait to find out what happens next."

"I remember." She reached down and stroked his penis, caressing the soft underside of his balls and enjoying the way the shaft jerked with each touch. He was very erect, the skin tight. A few drops of fluid pearled at the tip. She could easily make him come, taking him in her mouth or cradling him in her hand.

But that wasn't what she wanted—not yet. This evening was all about focusing on herself and her own pleasure. She wanted him to enjoy the time, as well, but not at her expense.

She crawled up his body, until she knelt over his mouth. She didn't even have to ask for what she wanted. He grasped her hips and dragged her closer, his mouth closing on her clit with a hunger that only increased her desire.

He was skilled and thorough, stroking, caressing, suckling with gentle pressure until she was trembling, a series of soft moans rising in volume from her throat. He reached up one hand and began fondling a breast, flicking his thumb across her nipple as his tongue did the same to her clit. The twin sensations sent her over the edge, to a climax stronger and more satisfying than any in memory.

When she began to feel too tender for his touch, she moved away, trailing her hands across his chest as she positioned herself over his shaft. She lowered herself onto him, inch by inch, and heard the hiss of his breath between his teeth when he was fully sheathed at last. He thrust upward, but his position beneath her and the movement of the hammock limited his range of motion. A fresh heat swirled through her at the realization that his climax truly depended on her and the moves she made.

She rose on her knees, then plunged onto him again, experimenting. He felt marvelous inside her, and her own climax had left her feeling euphoric. No wonder Passionata had been able to conquer ships, with this kind of energy at her disposal!

She glanced at Ian's face. His eyes were closed, his lips parted, every muscle tensed, much as he had looked when she had seen him yesterday in the hammock at his camp. The memory drove her to move faster, taking him in deeper, and she was delighted to find her own arousal growing. Every moment brought a fresh wave of sensation spiraling through her. Was this what all those women's magazines meant when they talked about the G-spot?

He made a hard thrust against her, and came with a loud cry. She held on, still moving over him, and was rewarded with her second climax shortly after. Ian reached up and pulled her into his arms and held her tightly. They lay for a long while, still connected, both breathing hard. He stroked her hair and smoothed his hand down her back. As if his fingers were the only part of him reluctant to be still.

They were in silvered darkness now, the last rays of sunset faded and a half-moon scarcely lightening the shadows. The tide was coming in, waves crashing against the rocks at the far end of the beach, drowning out the sounds of the tree frogs. Nicole smiled to herself, knowing this would be one of those moments imprinted on her memory forever—the sound of the waves, the smell of sex and salt, the feel of her bare breasts against Ian's chest and his hands stroking her hair. She wanted nothing to take away from this—no conversation or thoughts of the future.

So she pushed herself off him. When he started to protest, she put a silencing finger to his lips and bent to kiss his cheek. Then she stood, gathered her dress and panties and walked down the beach, leaving him to dress and make his way to his camp alone.

5

IAN TRIED TO CONCENTRATE on the notes he was making about the coral formations near Passionata's Island, but his mind continually fixed on thoughts of Nicole. What was she doing right now? Was she interested in doing *him* again—and how soon?

For a man who'd been accused of being led by his intellect, he could honestly say parts far south of his brain were running the show now. He'd told himself he'd come to the island to get in touch with his primitive side, but it had taken his encounter with Nicole to show him what that really meant.

The experience of sex for the sake of sex—focusing on the pleasure of the moment without the complicated, land-mine-littered dance of pursuit and courtship—had been wildly exhilarating.

But what had seemed so simple on the moon-washed beach proved more complex in the bright light of the next morning. What move should he make now? Clearly, Nicole was intent on calling the shots—a prospect he found equally frustrating and arousing.

He'd decided to wait a couple of days, to give her the opportunity to seek him out. After that, he was going after her. They had a long summer ahead of them, and he didn't want to waste any opportunities for a repeat of the previous night's ecstacy.

Meanwhile, he had work to do. He began to write once more:

A coral reef extends approximately one kilometer off the eastern shore of the island. This fine example of an untouched reef is home to an estimated four thousand species of fish, coral and other sea life, including the rare marble grouper and blue coral.

He put down his pen and frowned at the calm, academic language. What he really wanted to write was:

Only a brainless idiot would think dynamiting this reef and paving half the island to build a bloody naval air base was a good idea.

Unfortunately, the environmental group that was sponsoring this trip expected him to be more diplomatic. Scientific and intellectual. "We feel having a respected academic make our case for us will be more persuasive," Michael Penrod, the group's representative, had explained. "The government is accustomed to tuning out anyone they've labeled as an environmental extremist. We think they'll find science more difficult to ignore."

At first Ian hadn't believed Michael when he'd explained the British government had plans to build a military installation on Passionata's Island. He'd stared at drawings that called for blasting out the coral reef to provide a deep water port and bulldozing palm trees in order to lay down a concrete airstrip, and half believed this was someone's idea of a sick joke.

"It's very real," Michael had assured him. "They've kept very quiet about it in order to avoid alarming the public. But now we intend to raise a very loud alarm. Will you help us?"

Ian had readily agreed. Not only because Michael's group agreed to fund this summer of study that would allow him to complete his dissertation on Caribbean sea life, but also because he felt the government's plans were a violation of all that he had studied and worked for for so long.

He only hoped his dissertation, the photos he was taking and the narrative he would write, along with Michael's other plans, would encourage a normally complacent public to do something to stop the development. Would the average citizen care much about an uninhabited island thousands of miles away?

He hoped he could make them care.

Passionata's Island was a beautifully preserved paradise of marine life, and there was something very special about this place—a vibe Ian had felt from the first day he was here. The island was a world apart, a place where indulgences such as last night's encounter with Nicole seemed not only possible but inevitable.

So it was back to Nicole again. He shut his notebook and slotted the pen in the metal coils of its spine. Forget doing any more work today. He needed something to distract him completely.

Looking around, he spotted the paperback of *Confessions of a Pirate Queen* where he'd tossed it. Maybe reading would help him get his mind off Nicole.

Or else it would give him some ideas for their next encounter.

Two days after our initial encounter, I summoned William D. again. He stood before me, back straight, shoulders rigid, looking me in the eye. Captivity had not bowed him. But I could feel tension radiating from him.

"Remove his restraints," I ordered the guard who accompanied him.

She did as I instructed, then I dismissed her. When we were alone, I walked slowly around him, studying him, letting him feel my gaze on him. I visually traced the line of muscles along his back, the bulge of his arms and thighs. He was very strong—of body and of spirit. Exactly what I wanted in a man. A weak man was no challenge, and no fitting partner for the pirate queen.

I stopped in front of him once more. "How are you feeling?" I asked.

He glared at me, his anger impressive. The emotion aroused me all the more. "When are you going to let me go?" he demanded.

"You are my prisoner."

He was silent, making no answer, though if his eyes had been weapons, I would have been mortally wounded.

I moved closer, aware that I was taking a chance. I was sure part of him wanted me dead, but my loyal crew were stationed outside the door and would come to my aid at the smallest sound of distress. And, too, something in me sensed that William's hatred of me warred with another emotion equally as strong—the desire to experience all that I offered. "Have you been thinking of me?" I asked, trailing my hand lightly down his arm. "I've been thinking of you."

Still he made no answer, staring straight ahead.

I smiled and moved my hand down the hard plane of his chest, across the muscled ridges of his abdomen. Down to the harder ridge of flesh that filled his trousers. A thrill ran through me as I felt this evidence of his desire for me. "I see you *have* been thinking of me," I murmured.

I stepped back and looked at him until he shifted his gaze to look me in the eye. "Do you know why I sent you away the other day?"

He grunted. "You said I wasn't hard enough for you."

I nodded. "Physically you were aroused, but I wanted your mind engaged, as well. Did you know that the mind is the most powerful sex organ?"

I could see he was processing this information. He was clearly an intelligent man—another thing I require from any consort. "What are you going to do now?" he asked after a long silence.

"You need a bath," I announced, and rang the small brass bell that stood on a table nearby.

A servant appeared and I ordered hot water to fill the large zinc tub that had been placed at one end of the room. Towels were brought, as well as the lavender-scented soap I had made especially for my use.

When we were alone again, I turned to William. "Take off your clothes."

He hesitated, then did as I asked, removing the filthy garments. I would send them away to be burned.

When he was naked, I took a moment to appreciate him—the burnished tone of skin that had spent many hours in the hot sun, the pronounced muscle, the dark dusting of hair across his chest and at the crux of his thighs. And the erection standing proudly, straining toward me, quite thick and very hard. I felt a tightening in my womb, and a corresponding wetness between my thighs.

"Get in the tub."

He lowered himself into the water, a sigh of deep satisfaction escaping as the warm liquid enveloped him. I smiled at him and reached to undo the fastenings of my gown.

He grinned. "Are you going to join me?"

I stepped out of the gown, leaving me naked before him. His grin faded, replaced by a look of raw wanting that shook me. My nipples tightened under the caress of his gaze, and both my heartbeat and breath quickened. My desire for him was made all the more intense by the knowledge of how much he wanted me.

I knelt on the rug beside the tub, and picked up a soft sea sponge. "I may join you," I said. "But first, I will bathe you."

I scooped up a handful of the fragrant soft soap and

dripped it onto the sponge, then leaned forward and began to stroke it across his shoulders, down his arms, along his chest. I worked the sponge back and forth, creating a rich lather, smoothing away dirt and leaving his skin slick to the touch.

William said nothing, but his eyes never left me, and I was aware of the head of his penis poking above the water like a third eye watching me. Anticipating.

I brushed the sponge across his nipples, teasing them to erectness with the rough fibers. He made a small noise of pleasure in the back of his throat and shifted, sloshing the water out onto the rug. I pretended not to notice. "Lean forward so I may wash your back."

I rubbed the sponge up and down his back, in long, firm strokes, reveling in the perfection of his body. He gave another groan of pleasure and I set aside the sponge and began to use my fingers. Scooping up the rich lather, I worked my way down to his buttocks, grazing them with my nails, stroking soapy fingers along the cleft, listening to the quickening of his breath, watching the tension of his body and feeling a corresponding tension in my own.

I put my mouth close to him, and traced the curve of his ear with my tongue. "Lean back," I urged.

Again water sloshed over the edge of the tub, soaking my thighs, but I paid no heed. Again I washed his chest, using both hands, tracing each rib, plucking at his nipples.

He arched toward me, his hips rising up from the water, his engorged member brushing against my arm. I smiled, but ignored the gesture, and moved one hand down, and he lowered himself into the water once more.

I spent some time washing his legs and feet while he

watched with pained amusement in his expression. As I moved up between his legs his eyes lost some of their focus and his mouth slackened.

I lathered soap into his hair, and took pleasure in lathering his balls as well, the skin over them tight and silky in my hands. He was panting now. As I squeezed gently he let out a moan. "Are you determined to drive me mad?" he asked, his voice harsh.

"Mad for me, perhaps." I moved my hand up his shaft, and traced one finger around the tip. Blue veins stood out along the shaft, which pulsed with each movement of my hand. He strained toward me again, his eyes half-shut, muscles knotted with effort. I had never seen a more magnificent picture, and the knowledge that I alone had brought him to this thrilled me.

I began to move more deliberately, sliding my soapy hand up and down his shaft, applying a gentle pressure. My hand moved up, down, around—never still. I brought my other hand down to cup his balls, cradling them, feeling the skin around them draw up even tighter. I imagined the pressure within him, building almost to the breaking point, and let out a low moan.

He answered with a moan of his own, and came with a great thrust into my hand, the hot fluid mingling with the soap and water. I continued to stroke him, with great tenderness, until the spasms subsided. He sank into the water and stared at me with a look of awe and wonder. "What manner of woman are you?" he gasped.

I took my hands from him, and washed them in the water. "I am what every woman would be, if she only knew the possibilities."

NICOLE LAID ASIDE THE book and let out a deep breath. Wow. Passionata certainly had a way with words—and apparently with her hands as well. No wonder the press of the day had banned her writings.

She sat up and stared out at the empty expanse of ocean stretching beyond the inlet where the yacht was anchored. Would she ever have the courage to be as bold as the Pirate Queen? Her years of timidity had not brought her happiness, and she longed to try a new approach. But wanting and acting were two different things, though she vowed to use this interlude on the island to remake herself as much as possible.

Passionata had written that the brain was the most powerful sex organ. This wasn't a new idea to Nicole, but the Pirate Queen's method of engaging the brain as well as the body of her partner had certainly brought the point home.

Which led Nicole to her encounter with Ian on the beach last night. From the moment she'd decided to seduce him, all her senses had been heightened. Never had food been so flavorful or wine so intoxicating.

Watching him, knowing he was aware of her as well, had increased her fervor and fueled her imagination. When she'd led him to that hammock, she hadn't known exactly what she would do with him, only that she would follow her instincts, and in seeking her own pleasure, please him also.

The end result had been incredible, a combination, she was sure, of her own newfound freedom and daring, and the exotic moonlit setting. What could be more of a turn-on than a deserted moonlit beach in a tropical paradise?

She also couldn't fail to credit the man himself. Ian had been both a willing and active participant in the encounter. She'd known almost from their first meeting that he was aware of the physical attraction between them, and had accepted this as only natural. They were both young and single, with no commitments to anyone else. Given enough time alone, biology was bound to take its course.

She'd been surprised, then, when she'd looked into his eyes as she straddled him there in the hammock and felt the pull of another kind of connection. There in the semi-darkness, their bodies heated by intense physical desire, she'd recognized that Ian, like her, had come to the island searching for something. Not just treasure or a vacation, but something within themselves. Last night she felt she had touched on the thing she was seeking, some inner strength that would allow her to regain the confidence she'd lost in the aftermath of Kenneth's betrayal.

Her thoughts were interrupted by Adam's return. She heard the Zodiac's motor, and a few minutes later Adam heaved himself over the side of the yacht and dumped his scuba gear onto the deck. He glanced at Nicole. "What have you been doing with yourself all afternoon?"

"Reading." She held up the copy of *Confessions of a Pirate Queen.*

He grunted. "I can't believe you're still reading that book."

"You're the one who gave it to me."

He dropped into a deck chair. "I'd rather have you out there helping me than lying around here reading."

She resisted the urge to argue. He was clearly spoiling for a fight, and she wasn't going to give him the satisfaction. "I'll help when you really need me," she said calmly. "You assured me this morning you didn't. Why are you in such a bad mood?"

His shoulders slumped. "I haven't found a sign of anything. Not one single indication that the wreck of the *Eve* is anywhere around here."

Of course. Once Adam set his sights on something, he wanted it right away. "It's early days yet," she said. "That wreck has been undiscovered for almost 300 years—you can't expect to find it overnight."

He refused to be comforted. "I'm not some amateur casting about blindly in the ocean hoping to hit something," he said. "I've spent the better part of the year calculating the location of the wreck. And I was up half the night refiguring my calculations based on the information Ian gave me about the hurricane in 1850."

Yes, and bless him for staying occupied with his calculations while she went off with Ian. "You still can't be sure you're right," she said.

He glared at her. "I know I'm not wrong."

"Then you'll find the wreck. It's just going to take more time. You've got all summer."

"Which isn't all that long. Even once I locate an artifact, it could take weeks to bring it to the surface."

She held out her hands. "I don't know what to tell you. Except that you're not accomplishing anything fretting like this." She stood and patted his shoulder. "Maybe you should take a day off. Go fishing and let your mind rest. Do that and you're liable to come up with a fantastic solution to your problem—a better idea of where to look."

"Have I told you before how much I hate it when you're right?"

"Only because I learned from you. Do you remember when we were roommates and I was fretting about a difficult patient— the woman who refused to follow the dietician's guidelines and kept ending up back in the clinic with soaring blood sugar?"

He shook his head. "I don't remember."

"It doesn't matter. But you told me to forget about her for a while—to do something totally unrelated to her, and once I allowed my mind to relax, the perfect solution would pop into my head."

"And it worked?" He sounded skeptical.

She laughed. "Yes, it worked. I decided to cook a big dinner, and while I was in the kitchen I hit upon the idea of suggesting the woman hire a personal chef. She had the money, and hiring a chef felt like a luxury to her instead of the deprivation she viewed the dietician's guidelines as being. It worked out great for everyone."

He nodded. "Okay. So I'll go fishing tomorrow. What are you going to do?"

"Oh, I think I'll do a little hunting and gathering."

"Great idea. There are a lot of native foods here we should be taking advantage of. There's a guidebook around here somewhere you can use."

"Thanks." She'd take the guidebook, and maybe even collect some different foods to try. But the main focus of this particular hunting expedition would be a certain sexy British researcher. And once she'd located her quarry, she'd devote plenty of time to preparing him properly for another erotic encounter.

6

THE NEXT MORNING, AFTER Adam had dropped her on the beach and headed out in the Zodiac with his fishing gear, Nicole set off down the path through the jungle that led to Ian's camp. In the close confines of the dense foliage the air was thick and moist, smelling of greenery and decay. The light, filtered by the canopy of palm fronds and ferns, had a greenish hue, and gave Nicole the sensation of walking through a giant terrarium.

Beneath her feet the path was soft, and around her the foliage constantly stirred with the movement of small animals, birds and the land crabs that skittered behind every rock and under every fallen palm frond. And as she reached the clearing where Passionata's tower stood, she could hear the birds, their noise like that of rowdy soccer fans impatient for a game to begin.

Obviously, the island was not as deserted as she had first supposed. But at least the local wildlife had so far left her alone. She dashed across the clearing, then hurried on to Ian's camp. She was smiling when she stepped into the space he'd cleared out of the jungle for himself, remembering their last encounter.

She'd anticipated finding him there and was disappointed to discover the area deserted. The table beneath the open-fronted shelter was stacked with books, but the chair before it was empty, as was the hammock in the trees and the seating area around the fire pit. "Ian?" she called. Then louder. "Ian!"

But the only answer was the rattle of branches and the raucous cry of the birds.

Disappointed, she turned back toward the path, then hesitated. If Ian wasn't here, why not take a look around his camp? Try to learn more about the mysterious Englishman? If, as Adam suspected, Ian was also after the treasure, they'd be better off knowing for sure. Maybe he even knew something about the location of the wreck that would help them find it first. She was sure this was what Passionata would do. And after all, if she'd been more curious about Kenneth's life outside of their relationship, she might have saved herself a lot of heartache.

She glanced over her shoulder to make sure the coast was still clear, then hurried into the shelter. Constructed of the trunks of saplings lashed together and roofed with palm fronds, it was a sturdy and spacious protection from sun and rain. She examined the knots on the rope lashing and nodded in approval. Ian had done a good job.

Satisfied she'd learned all she could from the shelter itself, she focused on the books. The table was constructed of an old door balanced on several packing crates. She examined the titles of the books. *Foundations of Tropical Forest Biology, Green Imperialism, The Nature of Islands, Tropical Forage Plants.* Not what she'd term fascinating reading. There was, however, a well-worn copy of *Confessions of a Pirate Queen* in the stack. The reminder that Ian had read the same stories that had induced heavy breathing in her made her smile.

She picked up a sketch book and flipped through it. Colored pencil drawings of ferns, flowers and fish filled the pages. She studied a drawing of a delicate orchid. Not exactly Georgia O'Keeffe, but it was quite good.

She laid the sketch book back on the table. So far all she knew was that Ian had an interest in plants and animals and could draw. Oh, and that he was good with his hands. But she'd known that already, after last night.

She shuffled through the books once more and came across a leather-bound journal. Ah. This was more like it. Maybe now she could find out what Ian was really up to. She flipped to the first page and read.

I've been on the island exactly one hour and so far I've learned that the tower has been taken over by birds, who refuse to yield any ground. I've moved my camp a little further into the forest and have begun clearing space for a shelter. Other observations:

The land crabs will eat anything and everything left in the open or within their reach.

Cell phone doesn't work here. I figured as much, but thought it worth a try. I have the radio for emergencies.

Thank God for the solar chargers. The humidity is such here I predict batteries will corrode in a matter of days.

I have never felt so alone in my life. By the end of this trip I suspect I will know more about myself than I ever imagined possible. I can only hope the good revelations outweigh the bad.

What had the island revealed to Ian about himself so far? Were there dark secrets of his soul that had come to light on his first lonely nights here? Or unexpected resources within himself he hadn't expected to find?

Like her, had the island's history and romanticism, its exotic beauty and wild nature captured his imagination and made him want to experience that same wildness within himself?

"Finding anything interesting in there?"

She let out a scream and whirled around, colliding with Ian as he stepped into the shelter. He put his hands on her upper arms to steady her and looked into her eyes, his expression calm but cool.

She ducked her head and tried to compose herself. She stared down at his feet, which were clad in a pair of worn Tevas. He had well-shaped feet, with long toes, dusted with black hair. Masculine feet. Kind of sexy.

She jerked her head up, her breathing out of control once more. Her libido was in overdrive if she was getting turned on by feet!

"What were you doing reading my journal?" he asked.

She raised her chin. "Don't tell me if you came along and saw *my* diary lying out on a table with no one around, that you wouldn't take the opportunity to read it."

His left eye twitched, and he tightened his grip on her arms but not painfully so. He wasn't wearing a shirt, and she was aware of the slight sheen of sweat on his chest, and the way the muscles expanded when he took a deep breath. Standing this close to him, with only a few inches of humid air between their torsos, every part of her awakened to the memory of the feel of his body next to hers. Her nipples pebbled, and the muscles of her thighs tightened in a response as inevitable as a flower turning toward the sun.

Did she imagine the reluctance with which he released her and stepped back? But though his body moved, his eyes did not withdraw their gaze. "If there's something you want to know, why don't you ask me?" he said.

Asking was easy enough, but would he tell the truth? Some people—particularly some men, in her experience—had different ideas about what constituted the truth. But they'd get nowhere fast if she didn't at least take him up on his invitation.

"All right. What are you doing here on the island?"

He looked disappointed, as if he'd expected something more from her. "I told you." He nodded toward the books. "Research."

"You'd have been a lot more comfortable back home in the library," she said.

"Reading about something isn't the same as seeing it...as experiencing it."

His eyes met hers once more and she had a feeling they weren't necessarily talking about botany anymore. Was he remembering some of those passages from *Confessions of a Pirate Queen?*

Okay, keep your mind on the topic at hand. "So you came here to study plants and stuff?" she asked. "I saw your drawings, by the way. They were very good."

"Thanks. I did come here to study the local flora and fauna. But I also liked the idea of spending a summer relying on my own wits and resources."

Those words had the definite ring of truth. "So you're the rugged adventurer type." She smiled. "I might have known."

"Which is it that appeals to you most—the rugged or the adventurer part?"

She laughed. "Both. It's a nice change from men like my former boyfriend, the doctor. He considered himself an intellectual, above the common concerns of real life—or of anyone else but himself. And then, of course, Adam is a great guy, but he's only interested in two things—history and sailing." Either of them would have balked at the idea of a woman taking the lead in a relationship. Yet last night Ian had made no protest and didn't seem the least bit threatened by their encounter, though there was nothing of the weakling about him. In surrendering to her, he had made himself all the more masculine in her eyes.

He wasn't looking at her now, though. He was rearranging the books, stacking and restacking them, as though preoccupied with other thoughts. "Yeah. I guess everyone can be a little narrowly focused sometimes."

"It's nice to meet someone with a lot of different interests. Someone who's done things with his life."

She meant this as a compliment, but he didn't look pleased. "Was there something in particular you wanted from me?" he asked.

She gave him a long look, savoring a few of the possibilities that came to mind. She wanted him naked, she wanted him touching her, and she definitely wanted him inside her again. But they had a whole summer to spend together on this island. They couldn't be boinking their brains out the whole time. They should take the opportunity to get to know each other.

"I take it you know a lot about the plants that grow on this island," she said.

"I know a little about most of them."

"Then maybe you can help me. I'd like to supplement our food supplies." She held up the empty tote bag. "I have a book back on the yacht, but there's no substitute for having someone show you."

He nodded. "I can do that. When would you like to start?"

"Why not now? If you have time. Or did you have other plans for today?"

"Nothing that can't wait." He plucked a machete from a nail in one of the posts of the shelter and buckled the sheath around his hips, then donned a bushman's hat. He made a dashing figure, à la Indiana Jones.

Or Passionata's William D.

Just the man to follow her on an adventure of her choosing. An adventure she might never have imagined before she came to this place—this island still ruled by the legend of a pirate queen.

IAN LED THE WAY down the path from his camp, toward the beach on the opposite side of the island from the cove where

Adam's yacht was moored. Nicole followed close behind, the sweet floral perfume of the soap or the lotion she used rising up around him in the heat and wrapping him in an invisible embrace.

He quickened his steps, but he couldn't outrun the sense of being off balance that—along with outright lust—was his ever-present response to her. She was more unpredictable than any woman he'd ever known, constantly presenting a different face—from the domestic goddess who'd prepared dinner last night to the insatiable lover who'd straddled him in the hammock in the darkness.

Today, he had expected her to be coy about her presence in his camp. Instead, she'd readily admitted to snooping, seeming unashamed of her curiosity. Her openness had thoroughly defused his annoyance at finding her combing through his things.

There was nothing terribly incriminating there, anyway. He used the journal as a way of keeping track of the passing days and to record his observations about the environment on the island, with the occasional personal insight. Unless she had time to sit down and read the whole thing, he doubted she'd come to the conclusion that he was a frustrated academic on a quest to test his physical limits.

And apparently, she'd already made up her mind that he was some kind of he-man, out to conquer the world. He might have laughed at this assessment if she hadn't followed it up with her complaint about academics and intellectuals. So he'd buckled on his machete and set out to prove to her that yes, indeed, he was Indiana Jones, Robinson Crusoe, Jack Sparrow and any other fantasy man she desired rolled into one.

All in the name of her helping him fulfill a few fantasies of his own.

On this side of the island, the jungle extended almost to the ocean, with only a few yards of rocky coral between the thick vegetation and the choppy sea. Ian stopped at the edge of this growth and unsheathed the machete. "You probably already know about hearts of palm, right?" he asked.

"I've heard of them," she said. "But I don't know what they are."

He chose a small palm and sliced down into the center, then used the tip of the blade to dig out the tender green growth and showed it to her. "It's the new growth in the center—very tender and tasty with some kind of dressing on them."

She accepted the hearts of palm and tucked them into her tote bag. "I'll try them tonight. What else?"

He looked overhead, at the coconut palms arching over the ocean. "There's always coconuts."

She laughed. "This place is lousy with coconuts. But I have to admit, I never did much with coconut but eat it in cake or candy."

"Ah, then prepare to be educated." Grinning, he searched the ground until he found what he was looking for. He picked up the coconut and pointed to a green sprout emerging from one end. "Sprouting coconuts like this are different from the ones fresh off the tree." He laid the coconut on the ground and split it with one blow of the machete. Then he picked it up and opened it to show the creamy liquid center. "It's like pudding," he said. "Go ahead and taste it."

Looking skeptical, she scooped out a little of the contents with her fingers. Her skepticism changed to a smile. "Hey, this is pretty good."

He handed her the two halves. "Add that to your stash." He looked around and found a fresh coconut and handed her that also. "You can use coconut milk for almost anything you can use dairy milk for, including ice cream and in cooking."

She added the two coconuts to the bag. "You really do know your stuff."

"We're only just getting started." He led the way onto the beach. "You might get bored with the food on an island like this, but you'd never starve." Over the next half hour, he showed her sea purslane, sea grapes and a kind of edible seaweed, as well as mussel beds, crabs and several kinds of fish. Seldom had he had such an interested—and interesting—pupil, and it was difficult to resist the urge to lecture at length on a subject he knew so well.

"Let's stop and rest a minute," she said, sinking onto a rocky outcrop that extended out into the sea.

"Sure." He cursed himself for boring her with his long-winded oratory. She'd asked for a few pointers on native foods and he'd given her a graduate course overview.

But the smile she bestowed on him showed no annoyance. She patted the small patch of sand beside her. "Come sit here beside me."

He joined her, forced to sit very close in the narrow space. She leaned back and turned her face up to the sun, the breeze off the water ruffling her hair. Ian thought of a mermaid—or one of Passionata's pirates, luring sailors to their doom as they reclined on the rocks.

He was as willing to be lured as the next man. Or maybe she was waiting for him to make the first move. She had said nothing about last night, had not even acknowledged that anything unusual had happened. Was she waiting for him to say something or testing his patience—or what?

If she wanted action, he was more than willing to give it to her. He leaned toward her, intending to kiss her, when she said. "Tell me about your travels. Your adventures."

"My adventures?"

She glanced at him. "You must have been to a lot of interesting places, done exciting things. I mean, isn't that what you rugged outdoorsmen do?"

It was probably what rugged outdoorsmen did, but it wasn't necessarily what *he* did. Prior to coming to the island, he hadn't even been camping since he'd dropped out of Boy Scouts in the fifth grade. "I've spent most of the past few years in London," he said. He plucked at a small branch that had torn from a tree in some windstorm and come to rest on their rocky outcrop. "Nothing too exciting."

"Oh, come on." She nudged him. "You don't have to be modest with me."

He wasn't being modest, only truthful. But if he confessed he was merely a dull natural history student, she'd lump him in with those other men she'd found lacking.

Clearly he needed something to distract her, and he found it in the form of the branch in his hand. "Do you see this plant?" he asked, handing her one of the leaves.

She examined it. "Let me guess—if I boil it it will taste just like spinach." She handed it back to him. "I never cared for spinach."

He laughed. "No, it doesn't taste like spinach. It doesn't taste like much of anything, as far as I know. Anyway, it isn't the leaves that are useful. It's the bark."

"What's so special about the bark?"

"The tree is called Quebracho. It's bark contains yohimbe. It's considered an aphrodisiac."

She arched one eyebrow and studied the leaf again. "What does it do, exactly?"

"It's said to heighten sexual arousal and increase stamina." Come to think of it, the potion the Jamaican woman had sold him might have been concocted from this very species of plant.

She grinned. "Maybe we should try it."

He leaned closer. "Do you think we really need it?"

"I don't know." Her gaze met his, an intense look that sent an immediate jolt of heat straight to his groin. "Do you?"

He smoothed his hand down her arm. "When I'm with you, all I can think about is sex." He bent and kissed her neck, tasting the salt of her perspiration.

"I suppose that's something of a compliment," she murmured, arching to him.

"I meant it as such." He cupped her breast and continued kissing along the underside of her jaw. "You're a very sexy woman."

"Is it me, or is it this place?" She drew back enough to look him in the eye once more. "I think there's something about being here—where society's rules and conventions are so far away. It makes us...less inhibited. More daring."

He nodded. "I know what you mean. I feel it, too." He massaged her breast, rubbing the pad of his thumb across her erect nipple. "But I still say you're a very sexy woman."

"Mmmm." She made a sound of pleasure, then leaned forward and kissed him, openmouthed, her tongue tangling with his own.

Mouth locked to hers, he slipped his hand beneath her shirt, and beneath the bikini top she also wore.

She took hold of his wrist to stop him going further. "Let's not get carried away out here on this rock," she said. "There's not even enough room here to stretch out."

She was right, of course. This spit of sand scarcely wide enough for them both to sit was the only smooth surface in sight. All around them stretched rocky coral. There was the ocean, of course, which was fine for swimming, but one didn't want to let down his guard out there, since sharks were known to prowl the area. "Let's go back to my camp," he said. "I've got a very comfortable hammock. And we can always clear off the table."

She smiled. "Later." She turned to look out to sea. The wind had calmed and the ocean was a gray-blue expanse of glass, with a line of white ripples marking the edge of the offshore coral reef. Ian sucked in a deep breath of the salt-tinged air, trying to quell his frustration. No need to rush things. The two of them would be here all summer.

"If you could do anything you wanted with me right now, what would it be?" She was still staring across the water, a half smile on her lips. Her voice had a languid, dreamy quality.

"What do you mean?"

"I mean, if you could have your fantasy—whatever it is— what would it be?" She glanced at him. "Two women? Domination? Bondage?"

He had played with the idea of all these things in darker moments, but none of them held appeal in real life. So what *would* he like to do—with this woman, in this place?

He thought of their encounter last night—all it had been, and all it had not offered. "I'd undress you very slowly," he said. "In daylight, so that I could appreciate everything about you as I removed each item of clothing."

In his mind's eye, he could see himself slowly peeling off her T-shirt, then unbuttoning her shorts and sliding them down, inch by inch. "I'd take my time, getting to know every part of you. I'd run my tongue over your collarbone, down the hollow of your throat. I'd watch your nipples harden and pucker at my touch and stroke the soft skin over your belly while you writhed beneath me."

His voice was rough, and he was surprised at how difficult it was to talk about these things. He felt…almost silly. Sex wasn't a subject for conversation, it was something he did.

But he could see how his words were a turn-on for her. Her pupils enlarged and her breath became rapid and shallow. He shifted beside her to accommodate his growing erection.

"Go on," she said. "What would you do next?"

He closed his eyes, thinking. "When we were both naked, I'd lay you down and spread your legs. I'd part the folds of your clit and see how wet you were."

She smiled. "I think I'd be very wet."

He imagined she was wet right now, just from him talking to her. Is this what Passionata had meant, when she'd written of engaging their minds as well as their bodies in the experience of sex?

He leaned closer to her, pressing his body against hers. "I'd want to taste you. I'd stroke your clit again and again with my tongue. I'd bring you to the edge, but I wouldn't let you come."

"You wouldn't?"

"Not yet. I'd wait until we were both half-mad with waiting, and then I'd let you go, in a spectacular climax."

She said nothing, but she was breathing heavily now. He put his mouth to her ear and sucked the earlobe into his mouth. "That would only be the first time. I'd make you come again. And again."

She turned and wrapped her arms around him and kissed him, plunging her tongue deep into his mouth, her breasts pressed against his chest. They kissed feverishly, as though this contact alone would be enough to ease their frustration. She smoothed her hands across his bare chest, around to his back. He was thinking of risking the sharks and dragging her into the ocean when a shout startled them both.

They wrenched apart and, heart pounding, he stared down the beach. Adam strode toward them from the Zodiac he'd beached farther down. He was scowling and his fists were clenched.

Nicole swore under her breath, and rose to her feet. Ian scrambled up after her. "You're sure he's not your boyfriend," he said.

She shook her head. "I promise he isn't."

"It's just that he doesn't look too happy to see us. Or rather, to see me."

"Don't worry about him." She hopped across the short expanse of water separating them from the main line of beach and strode down the rock toward her shipmate.

Ian ran along beside her. "You're interrupting us," he said, wanting to take the offensive, and bristling at the idea that Nicole might feel the need to defend him.

Adam scowled. "So I saw." He turned to Nicole. "You need to come back to the ship, right away."

Her expression changed from anger to concern. "Why? Is something wrong?"

"Nothing's wrong."

"Then what is it?"

Adam glanced at Ian, clearly unwilling to talk in front of him. "I'll tell you later."

Nicole crossed her arms over her chest and glared at him. "You can tell me now."

He shook his head. "I don't think so."

"This is ridiculous," she said. "We're the only three people on the island. Ian isn't stupid. He's going to figure out what you're up to sooner or later. You might as well tell him."

"What you're *up to?*" Ian looked from her to Adam. Were they running drugs or something? "What's going on here?"

Adam only scowled at him. Nicole let out a huff of exasperation and turned to Ian. "When Adam isn't teaching history to undergrads, he's an amateur treasure hunter."

"So he's here hunting treasure?" He'd heard rumors of pirate treasure, but had supposed they weren't based in fact. After all, what was a pirate story without buried treasure?

"Adam thinks he knows the location of the *Eve,* Passionata's pirate ship, that sank off the coast of the island in 1714."

"You didn't know about the ship?" Adam asked.

Ian shook his head. "No. So you've found it?"

Again, Adam was silent. Nicole leaned over and shoved him. "What did you come here to tell me?" she asked. "Is it something about the treasure? I thought you were going fishing today."

"I did," he said. "But I caught more than fish." He reached into his pocket and retrieved what at first appeared to be a blackened disc. It lay in his palm, a misshapen lump.

"What is it?" Nicole asked.

"It's a gold coin." Adam held the disc up to the light. "Part of Passionata's treasure."

7

IAN STUDIED THE BLACKENED DISC. It was misshapen, encrusted with grime and sand. Certainly not something he had ever seen before in the sea, but was it really valuable?

"That's a gold coin?" Nicole asked. "How would you ever know?"

"It's a coin that's been underwater three hundred years, but look." Adam unsnapped the knife from his belt and scraped the blade across the surface of the disc. A streak of gold glinted in the bright sunlight.

"Where did you find it?" Ian asked. "Was this the only one?"

Adam looked at him, as if debating whether to answer the question. "It's the only one I have now," he said after a moment. "But I'm sure there are more."

"Where did you find it?" Nicole asked.

"It was in one of the fish I caught. I put out a marker so I can find the spot again."

"So you think there are more coins like this?" Ian asked.

"Not only coins, but other things, too," Nicole said.

Adam scowled at her. "Nicole—"

"Passionata's treasure," Ian said, recalling Adam's announcement when he'd first showed the coin to them. "You mean there really is a buried treasure?"

"Not buried, exactly," Nicole said. "It's a shipwreck. The

wreck of Passionata's own ship, the *Eve*. Do you mean you didn't know?"

He shook his head.

"Then what are you doing here alone, diving every day, if you're not looking for the treasure?" Adam asked.

"He's already told you," Nicole said. "He's working on a book."

He'd never said that, exactly, but let her think that, if she wanted. The truth was much less exciting.

"So you haven't been looking for the wreck of the *Eve*," Adam said.

"I never even knew it existed." He looked at the coin in Adam's hand. "You think the wreck is near where you caught this fish? Couldn't the fish have swallowed the coin anywhere?"

"I've spent the past year studying journals, contemporary accounts of the wreck, sailor's diaries, current patterns, even satellite images, pinpointing the most likely spot for the wreck," Adam said. "But when I dove there, I found nothing. Then you mentioned that hurricane in 1850 and I realized I hadn't allowed for the violence of a storm like that. It could have repositioned the entire wreck. On the way here I was running through my calculations again in my head, and I think the area where I caught the fish that contained this coin is the right place to look for the *Eve*."

"What do we do now?" Nicole asked.

"Tomorrow I want to make a dive," Adam said. "See what else we can find."

"I can help," Ian said.

Adam scowled at him and started to refuse, but Nicole intervened. "That's a good idea," she said. "We can work faster with three of us."

Adam's demeanor didn't change. "What's your interest in this?" he asked.

Ian shrugged. "It would be good to have something else to do with my time," he said. "I'm getting pretty bored sketching plants and photographing fish."

"Is that what you're doing with your time?" Adam asked.

"Mostly." When he wasn't making out with Nicole. Or thinking about making out with her.

"Adam, we need the help," Nicole said. "We should accept Ian's offer."

"All right," Adam said grudgingly. He pocketed the coin. "Meet us at the yacht tomorrow morning at sunrise. I want to get started as soon as it's light enough to see."

"All right."

He glanced at Nicole. *What now?* was his silent question. Was she going back to the yacht with Adam?

She slipped her arm into his. "I'll walk you back to your camp," she said.

Ian's spirits lifted. And when they reached camp, they would pick up where they'd left off before Adam interrupted....

"Where do you think you're going?" Adam asked.

"Back to Ian's camp."

"We have things to do to get ready for tomorrow. We have to check all the dive equipment, ready the cameras—"

She waved away his words. "We have plenty of time to do that. I'll be there soon enough."

Then she turned away, tugging Ian toward the path that led back to his camp.

"What's his problem?" Ian asked when they were in the jungle once more. "Are you sure he's not jealous, or is he like this with everyone?"

"He's like this with everyone. I told you, he has a two-track mind—history or sailing. This treasure-hunting hobby encompasses both. He's fixed on a goal and assumes everyone else is just as focused."

"Why did you come on the trip, then?"

"He needed someone to crew the yacht and I needed something to do." She glanced at him. "I've sailed with him before, so I'm used to his moods. And I wanted to use this time to decide where to go next with my life."

He nodded. Hadn't he thought much the same thing about his visit to the island? "Maybe if more people had a chance to take a time-out like this, everyone would be happier," he said.

Her smile had a heat he felt to his core. "It should be a law. Every adult gets three months to experiment with his or her life—try on different roles, test theories, question the status quo, and see if a different lifestyle feels better to them."

"Is that how you see your time on the island—an experiment?" He could see the appropriateness of the term, though it wasn't one he'd have used.

She snuggled closer to him. "I intend to do things I would never have the chance to do in my ordinary life. Including—" she paused to kiss the side of his neck "—having lots of hot and...*experimental* sex with you."

"Right." He cleared his throat. "Sounds great." He only hoped he had the energy and imagination to keep up.

NICOLE LOVED THE WAY a word or a look from her could throw off Ian's solid, masculine calm. Outwardly he was like so many men she'd known: intelligent, unemotional, almost stoic—methodical and confident of his role in male/female interactions. Translation: they were used to being in charge, and the idea that it could be any other way caught them off guard.

But Ian had been surprisingly open to her suggestions. Maybe, like her, he saw the appropriateness of using this island interlude for experimentation. Or maybe he was ready for something different in his life.

When they reached his encampment, she looked around. "What do you think?" she asked. "The hammock or the table?"

He gave her an appraising look, a hint of a smile at the corners of his mouth. "We used a hammock the other night."

"Then the table it is." Appreciating the effectiveness of a dramatic gesture, she swept the books into the sand and hopped up on the table. "You talked about undressing me," she said. "But I think you should undress for me first."

"Oh you do, do you?"

She folded her arms beneath her breasts. "Yes, I do."

His gaze zeroed in on the deep cleft between her breasts. "Are you sure you don't want to do it my way?"

His way—as he'd described on the beach—indeed sounded pleasurable. But she enjoyed shaking things up and had found the results, so far, extremely gratifying. "I want to see you naked," she said, and crossed her legs.

He shrugged, and with one swift movement, unbuttoned his shorts and shoved then to his ankles, along with his underwear. He kicked out of them and his sandals. Time elapsed: approximately three seconds. Not the sensual striptease she'd hoped for, but probably what she should have expected.

The important thing was he was now naked, and he was definitely one of the more attractive nude men she'd seen. That day she'd spied on him in his hammock, she hadn't appreciated the narrowness of his waist or the tautness of his backside.

"Now it's your turn." He stalked toward her, his erection bobbing with each deliberate step. His movements were unselfconscious, with that touch of male arrogance and body confidence that seemed innate to the gender. It was one of the most irritating things about men—and one of the most appealing.

His hands on either side of her thighs on the table, he leaned in to kiss her—a slow, sensual pressure of lips and tongue that sent heat spiraling through her. She pressed her palms flat against his chest, his skin warm beneath her cool fingers. Then she shoved him away, gently, and reached for the top button of her blouse.

He grinned and settled back to watch the unveiling. Aware of his gaze on her, she took her time, undoing each button as slowly as possible, pushing aside the fabric of the shirt as if she was uncovering an elegant gift—which, of course, he should consider her to be.

When the shirt was removed, she reached back to unfasten the clasp of her bikini top. Then she stopped and grinned at him, teasing, and traced one forefinger along the neckline of the top. "Are you sure you want to see?"

"I'd hate for that top to be destroyed when I rip it off you," he said.

The threat—which had no heat behind it, she was sure—sent a flood of arousal straight to her sex. She unfastened the clasp, then slipped the top off over her head.

Before she had time to react, he swooped in, fastening his mouth to one breast with a fierceness that stole her breath. For a split second, she thought of demanding that he wait, but the action of his lips and tongue left her speechless, squirming. He transferred his attention to her other breast, one hand caressing her waist.

Part of her brain insisted that Passionata wouldn't have put up with this attempt to usurp her control. She'd have ordered William D. to back off and made him pay for his insolence.

The rest of her brain told this part to get stuffed. She was enjoying what Ian was doing to her too much to protest—that is, if she could have done more than utter incoherent moans and sighs.

Somehow in the midst of all his attention to her breasts, he stripped off her shorts and the bikini bottoms, and her sandals. He spread her thighs wide, fondling and caressing, but never quite touching her sex, which pulsed with the slightest breeze across her fevered core.

Attempting to regain some control, she slipped her legs around his waist and drew him close, locking her ankles to hold his erection pressed against her aching clit. He tried to move away, but she had him trapped, his struggles only succeeding in increasing their arousal.

She looked up at him, a surge of triumph running through her. "What should we do now?" she asked.

He leaned in and kissed her again. After the urgency of their movements until now, the tenderness of the gesture stirred her. A yearning rose in her chest that had nothing to do with physical desire, and the intensity of the emotion frightened her. This experiment with Ian wasn't about emotional intimacy. Her goal was to build her self-confidence, to feel empowered and to have a lot of fun. She didn't want to feel this softness toward him—this vulnerability.

Heart pounding, she broke off the kiss and turned away, not wanting him to read her thoughts in her eyes. She arched toward him, provocatively. "Interesting how this table is the perfect height," she said. "Did you plan it that way?"

He slipped his hands beneath her thighs and tugged her forward, so that the tip of his erection was poised right at her entrance. "I planned it that way. Took measurements and everything."

She laughed and felt safe looking at him once more. "We'd better test it thoroughly, just to make sure."

At this, he thrust into her, filling her completely, pleasure radiating through her. "That feels amazing," she gasped, even as he began to move out of her again.

He pulled almost completely out of her, then thrust forward again, establishing a rhythm that soon had her poised on the edge of release. She squirmed beneath him, trying for a better angle, and silently cursed every mythical woman—she knew none personally—who could supposedly climax with vaginal stimulation alone.

"Finger me," she growled at him.

"What?" He glanced at her, clearly distracted.

She grabbed his hand and dragged it into her mouth, and licked his thumb and forefinger, then forced them down to her clit. "Finger me," she said again.

"Like this?" He dragged his thumb across her clit, pressing firmly, watching her face as he continued his deliberate thrusts.

"*Yessss.*" She leaned back and closed her eyes, losing herself in the exquisite combination of sensations.

He stroked more firmly, both within and without, and his breathing became more labored. But she was only dimly aware of him, concentrating as she was on the tightening of her own muscles and the pressure building within.

One hard thrust sent her over the edge, heat and light flooding her in a beautiful release. With a guttural cry, he came also, the table dancing backward with these final movements.

She put her arms around him, and he embraced her and kissed the top of her head and the side of her face. "I'd say that was a successful experiment," he said, a little breathless.

She laughed, relieved he hadn't said something serious. Anything but a lighthearted approach would spoil everything. She leaned back and looked at him. "I definitely think we should continue our experiments, early and often."

"Absolutely," he said with mock solemnity. "Anything in the name of science."

IAN HAD NEVER FOUND anything graceful about the denouement of any sexual encounter, but with Nicole he found it easy to be relaxed, to joke, even, as they cleaned up and dressed again. It helped that she didn't feel the need to critique his performance or question him about hers. She neither waxed sentimental nor behaved as if sex was a chore or something to be sandwiched between dinner and that evening's television viewing.

As he slipped into his sandals once more, it occurred to him that these observations proved he'd been hanging out with the wrong women. For one thing, he'd never had a woman take charge of a relationship the way Nicole had. Objectively he thought his masculinity ought to be threatened, but realistically he was flattered, and aroused at the idea that all the responsibility for the success or failure of the encounter did not lie with him.

Danielle had complained that he lived inside his head, but she had never once explained what she wanted him to do instead. Sex had always been at his instigation, and too many times he had felt he was doing all the work.

With Nicole, her focus seemed to be on her own pleasure, but so far he hadn't felt slighted.

"I'll walk you back to the beach," he said.

"Thanks." She flashed another of her brilliant smiles. "I'll admit walking through the jungle by myself creeps me out a little. I'm afraid something nasty is going to drop onto my head."

He laughed and handed her her totebag. "Don't forget dinner."

She peeked into the bag again. "Hearts of palm salad, braised purslane and coconut pudding. Should be a gourmet meal. Want to join us?"

"I'm tempted, but I'd better take a rain check. I have work I need to do tonight." Not to mention an evening spent with the glowering Adam wasn't his idea of a great time.

They found Adam kneeling on the deck of the yacht, diving equipment arranged around him. He glanced up as they climbed onboard, then said, "Bring your camera tomorrow, Marshall. We'll want to photograph anything we find before we move it.

And be sure and wear gloves. No sense getting cut on coral or a piece of sharp metal."

"I'm glad you're so concerned for my welfare," Ian said as he squatted down next to a hand-held underwater spotlight.

"He just doesn't want to waste time stopping to patch you up," Nicole said. She sat cross-legged between them and inspected a weight belt.

Adam ignored their teasing and continued his instructions. "If we find anything, we leave it where it lays. Photograph it. Set a marker. Depending on the object, we'll decide whether or not to try to bring it to the surface and how to do so."

"Are you worried about oxidation?" Ian asked. "Do some things fall apart when exposed to the air?"

Adam nodded. "It can happen. We also don't want to salvage more than I can comfortably transport back to the States."

Ian looked around the yacht. "And how much is that?"

"Not much," he admitted. "My goal is to recover a few choice items as proof of the find, and use them to generate enough interest for a grant or private funding to return next summer to launch a full-scale salvage operation."

"How much money does something like that take?" Ian asked.

"Why? Do you have a few million you'd like to contribute?"

Ian shook his head. Thanks to a small inheritance from an uncle, and some lucky stock picks, he had enough to live comfortably, but not the kind of funds Adam was obviously seeking.

Adam stood and surveyed the scattered equipment. "I've checked everything. We should be able to get an early start in the morning." He stared out over the water. "I won't sleep tonight, knowing we're this close and still have to wait."

"We may have to wait even longer," Nicole said.

Both men turned to her. "What are you talking about?" Adam demanded.

She pointed toward the horizon. "We've got company," she said.

Ian blinked. He thought at first he was imagining things, but no, those were sails approaching, and getting nearer. A yacht, slightly larger than Adam's, was making its way toward Passionata's island.

8

ADAM AND IAN TOOK ADAM'S Zodiac out to help secure the mooring lines of the new arrival. When they hailed the ship, Ian was startled to see his friends, Bryan and Michelle Peachtree. "Didn't expect to see us here, did you?" Bryan asked with a laugh.

"We thought you might be getting lonely and wanted to surprise you," Michelle added.

When the Peachtrees' yacht was secured and everyone convened on shore, Ian made the introductions. "So you're spending the summer here, as well?" Bryan said. "For a deserted island, this place gets a lot of traffic."

"Yes, it does." Once again Adam's expression communicated his viewpoint.

"It's always nice to meet new people," Nicole countered.

"I'm glad Ian's had company," Michelle said.

"Yes, I was half-afraid we'd find you running around like a wild man, out of your head after having no one to talk to and nothing to eat but fish and coconuts," Bryan said.

"I'm not reduced to that yet," Ian said dryly.

"We've brought you some supplies," Michelle said. "Meat and fresh vegetables."

"And booze," Bryan added.

"We'll have to celebrate." Ian turned to Nicole and Adam. "Have dinner with us tonight at my camp."

"I won't say no to that," Adam said.

Nicole took hold of Adam's arm. "We'll let you all visit and we'll see you tonight. It was nice meeting you."

"Come see my camp," Ian said to his friends.

"I'm curious as to how you're managing," Bryan said. He and Michelle followed Ian down the narrow jungle path. He looked around at the dense growth. "This place is more primitive than I imagined."

"It's creepy," Michelle said as she batted a spiderweb out of her way. "Do those birds always carry on this way?"

"They quiet down at night." Ian had to shout to be heard over the clamor of the birds as they reached the tower clearing.

"What's this?" Bryan asked, also raising his voice.

"It supposedly was built as the headquarters for Passionata. You remember, the female pirate in that book you gave me?" Ian said. "If you like, we can explore it later. But you'll need to wear a hat."

"I can see that." The three hurried across the clearing and into the jungle on the other side.

"Is there a reason your camp is so far from the other couple?" Michelle asked.

"They arrived after me," he said. "I set up closest to the reef so it would be more convenient for study, while the best place for anchoring ships is on the other side of the island."

"Nicole is one fine-looking woman," Bryan said.

"And her boyfriend looks quite formidable," Michelle added.

"Adam isn't her boyfriend," Ian said. "Just an old friend."

"And you know this how?" Bryan asked as they emerged at Ian's camp.

Ian ignored the question and gestured to the camp. "Here we are. Home sweet home."

"You did all of this?" Michelle entered the hut and surveyed the table and the shelter's stout construction.

"This is impressive." Bryan grinned and turned in a slow circle, taking in the entire campsite.

"Let's sit down and I'll fix you a drink," Ian said. "Although all I have is water or coconut water."

"I'll have coconut water, whatever that is." Bryan sat on one of the stumps that served as chairs around the cold fire pit. Michelle sank gracefully to the sand at his feet.

Ian retreated to the shelter and returned shortly with three glasses hollowed from thick bamboo, filled with the slightly sweet coconut water.

Bryan took a sip. "Not bad," he observed. "Would be even better with gin."

"I've been thinking of experimenting with making some kind of coconut vodka or beer," Ian said. "But I haven't gotten around to it yet."

"This setup is amazing," Bryan said. "I didn't know you had it in you. Frankly, I kept expecting to hear you'd radioed for relief within the first week."

"He insisted we sail out here to find out what happened to you," Michelle said.

"I was sure you were either dead or gone bonkers," Bryan said.

"Nice to know my friends have so much confidence in me." Ian didn't attempt to conceal his annoyance.

"Mind you, I'm relieved to find you doing so well," Bryan continued. "But you must admit, one doesn't expect a man whose previous chief experience with the outdoors consisted of watching nature videos on TV and the occasional field trip to collect specimens to turn out to be a regular Robinson Crusoe."

"Don't mind him," Michelle said. "He's green with envy at the idea of you spending the summer in a tropical paradise while he's stuck teaching overindulged schoolboys."

"So how did you manage to get away?" Ian asked. "And where did you get that yacht? I didn't even know you sailed."

"First summer term is over and I declined to be enslaved for the second term," Bryan said. "The yacht belongs to a friend of the Fund for the Rescue of the Earth's Environment. I persuaded him to lend it to me in exchange for a progress report from you."

Ian shook his head. Bryan had always had a golden tongue, able to talk perfect strangers into the most amazing things. "You can report back to FREE that I'm doing well," he said.

Bryan's expression sobered. "They really want a report from you," he said. "And any pictures, specimens, video—anything you can supply them. Things are moving forward with plans for the airstrip at a much more rapid pace than they'd anticipated."

"I can certainly send a report and pictures," Ian said. "They don't want me to come back to Britain already, do they?" He felt a pang of regret at the idea. He wasn't ready to leave paradise just yet.

"They didn't say anything about that," Bryan said. "Only that they wanted to get started planning their media attack."

"This is such a wild place," Michelle said. "I can't say I like it, but I'd hate to see it paved over and industrialized."

"It would be a crime," Ian said with fervor. "I've found at least a dozen rare species of plants and animals here, a couple of which may be unique to this island. Not to mention the abundant birdlife and the rich history of the place—"

"Hold on," Bryan held up his hand. "You don't have to convince me." He leaned forward and studied his friend. "You're really loving it here, aren't you?"

Ian nodded. "I am." For the first time in his life, he'd been forced to rely on his own strengths and resources. The island had helped him discover depths to himself he hadn't known before. And he was making new discoveries every day.

"I don't see how you stand it here without e-mail and cell phones and television," Michelle said. "You don't even have radio."

"It was a little tough adjusting at first," Ian admitted. "But there are compensations."

"And would the delectable Nicole be one of those compensations?" Bryan asked with a leer.

Michelle pinched her husband's leg. Bryan let out a yelp, but his grin never faded. He drained his glass, then stood. "We'd better get back to the ship and settle in a bit before supper," he said.

"We'll bring the food and drinks over here about six, if that's all right," Michelle said, standing also.

"You'd better bring plates and cups, too," he said. "I only have a couple of each."

"We'll bring everything we need for dinner, then—from the food to pots to cook it in and plates to serve it on," Michelle said.

"That sound great," Ian said. "You might give a shout out to Adam and Nicole when you head over here. We don't go by clocks much around here."

"Before we go, I have some letters for you." Bryan reached into the pocket of his shorts and drew out two envelopes and handed them to Ian.

He glanced at the addresses. The first letter was from Michael Penrod with FREE. The second was written in a familiar feminine handwriting. "It's from Danielle," he said, surprised.

"Not good news, I'm afraid," Bryan said. "Not that I've read the letter, but I suspect she's writing to tell you she's getting married."

"Bryan!" Michelle scolded.

He glanced at his wife. "He's going to find out soon enough. If I was in his shoes, I know I'd rather hear it from a friend."

Danielle—married? Ian tried to absorb the idea, but it stayed stubbornly on the surface of his emotions. "He's right," Ian said. "I would rather hear it from a friend." He stuffed both envelopes into the pocket of his trunks and assumed a cheerful expression. "Not that it matters. I wish her happiness."

"That's the spirit." Bryan punched him on the shoulder. "She wasn't good enough for you, you know."

Ian felt a sudden surge of emotion as he looked at his friend. Ian could see that underneath his good-natured ribbing and feigned predictions of Ian's inability to survive on the island, Bryan really had been worried. He'd given up a semester's income and probably gone to considerable trouble to obtain use of the yacht in order to reassure himself of Ian's safety.

Ian clapped his friend on the shoulder. "It's good to see you, Bry. I'm glad you made the trip out here."

"It's good to see you looking so well." Bryan's grin widened. "We'll celebrate in style tonight. Steak and gin. And tomorrow you can show me around your island paradise."

"We'll do that," Ian agreed. "One more thing before you go. Don't say anything to Nicole or Adam about what I'm doing here—the doctoral research or my work for FREE."

"They don't know about that?" Michelle asked. "Then what did you tell them?"

"I let them think I'm writing a book. That I came here for the adventure."

"Do they have something against environmental crusaders?" Bryan asked. "Or doctoral students?"

Ian didn't know how to explain his reluctance to reveal his background to Nicole without sounding foolish. Probably the less said the better. "I have my reasons," he said. "Will you promise to keep mum?"

Michelle nodded. "We can do that." She nudged her husband. "Can't we?"

"As far as I'm concerned, you're the original mystery man. Mum's the word."

The couple departed and when Ian was alone again he retreated to the shelter and sat in the shade, the two letters laid out on the table before him. He debated which to read first, then picked up the one from Danielle.

In sprawling, rather sloppy handwriting, she greeted him and made the usual polite inquiries about his health. Then she got right to the point.

> I wanted you to know I'm getting married next month. By the time you return to England, I will be Mrs. Charles Grayson. Or, as he's known by his legion of fans, Charlie G. I imagine you'll see me next fall on the television, standing on the sidelines, cheering him on to victory.

So she'd snagged her rugby player for good. He didn't miss the smug tone of her words, the way she pointed out that her husband-to-be had fans. He was famous enough to be featured on television.

He was the rugged he-man Ian would never be.

He laughed out loud and put the letter away, something very like relief flooding him. What a bullet he'd dodged with Danielle, he thought to himself. He'd wasted too much time trying to make her happy, while she'd struggled to make him over into something he wasn't.

How much better to have a woman who looked out for her own happiness and didn't try to change him.

A woman like Nicole.

He quickly pushed the thought away. He and Nicole were having fun together, but there was no future in their relationship. It was a diversion to be enjoyed here on the island. A fantasy as fun and transient as their time in paradise.

He slit open the second envelope. This letter was typed, the black ink against the white paper adding to the urgency of the words. Phrases jumped out at Ian: "government moving forward on its request for funding," "surveying could begin as early as this fall," "contractors already lining up to bid…"

Then, a note below:

"We are preparing to launch an all-out media campaign to arouse public sentiment—and indeed world sentiment—against this project. Any photographs and other documentation you can provide will be invaluable to us both now and in the future."

He folded the letter, replaced it in the envelope and carefully filed it in the back of his notebook. Before he'd come here, he'd believed intellectually in the wrongness of the government's plans to build an airbase on the island. Now, after only a short time living here, he knew what a crime it would be to destroy such a rare, unspoiled place. He would do everything in his power to prevent that from happening.

NICOLE DRESSED CAREFULLY for the party that evening in a batik sarong she'd picked up in Jamaica and a necklace of tiny shells she'd purchased from a vendor on the beach at Ocho Rios. As she fussed with her hair and makeup, Adam paced the small cabin. "We've got to convince these two Brits to leave the island as soon as possible," he said.

"Why would we want to do that?" She looked over her shoulder at them. "They've brought food and liquor, which they're willing to share. They're friends of Ian's, and they seem like nice people. Why are you so anxious to get rid of them?"

Adam stopped and stared at her, as if he couldn't believe her stupidity. "We can't dive for the treasure as long as they're here."

"Why not?"

"Because they'll want to know what we're up to. And I don't want anyone knowing about this find until I've secured financing."

"You're going to have to tell someone to get the money, aren't you?" Nicole turned back to the mirror and swept a second coat of mascara across her lashes.

"I'm going to see if the Peachtrees will take a letter for me back to a colleague of mine in the States," Adam said. "One with the right connections to get the funding I need."

"So you're willing to take advantage of Bryan and Michelle's visit to the island, you just don't want them to stick around," she said.

He grunted and resumed pacing. Nicole slipped on earrings and was finally ready. "Let's go before you wear a hole in the floorboards."

Bryan and Michelle had hailed them half an hour ago on their way to Ian's camp, so she knew they were already there. Unlike Adam, Nicole was pleased with the addition of Ian's friends to the island's population. Not that life on the island had grown dull, but new faces with news of the outside world were exciting, and the prospect of a party only added to the festive air.

Ian, perhaps already feeling the effects of the bottles of gin and vodka sitting on the table that had been dragged nearer the fire pit, greeted them warmly, shaking Adam's hand and kissing Nicole's cheek. He'd decorated for the occasion, with lit candles stuck in shells flickering from all around the shelter and rock niches surrounding the camp.

"Take a seat, and I'll fix you a drink," Bryan, playing the role of bartender, said. "We've got coconut water and gin or vodka, gin and tonic or martinis."

"A martini, please," Nicole said.

"Same for me." Adam took a seat nearest the bar. "Thanks for inviting us over," he said, apparently prepared to play the gracious guest in spite of his earlier complaining.

Bryan made drinks and distributed them, then sat on the edge of the table/bar. "So what brings you two to Passionata's Island?" he asked Adam.

"We're here for the diving," Adam took a long swallow of the martini and smiled appreciatively. "That goes down good."

"I'll bet you were surprised to find Ian already here," Bryan said.

Adam shrugged. "Though the island's uninhabited, it's on most maps. I guess it's not that unusual for people to check it out."

"Too bad you don't dive," Ian said. "The reef is pretty spectacular. I've taken some amazing photographs of fish and coral."

"I'd like to see those," Bryan finished his own drink and turned to make a refill. "Anybody discovered any pirate's treasure or anything interesting like that?"

With his back to them, Bryan didn't see Adam's face turn red. He made choking noises and Nicole pounded his back. Ian covered for them well, laughing heartily. "People think every island in the Caribbean has buried treasure on it," he said. "No one ever finds anything."

"But this island really was inhabited by a pirate, wasn't it?" Bryan said. "This Passionata?" He laughed. "What a name! It sounds like something from a romance novel—although from what I remember, that book she wrote was pretty racy stuff."

"As far as I know, Passionata never buried any treasure," Ian said.

Nicole smiled at him, sending a silent thank-you for keeping their secret. Of course, technically, Passionata's treasure wasn't *buried*. It was only resting under thousands of gallons of seawater.

"Let's go ahead and grill the steaks," Michelle said. "I'm starved."

They readily agreed, and in a few minutes five thick rib-eyes were cooking on a grill over the campfire, while foil-wrapped potatoes baked in the ashes. Nicole's mouth watered at the smell of the sizzling beef. Though they hadn't been on the island long enough to truly feel deprived, the prospect of a summer of canned meat and fish had been daunting.

Over the delicious meal, and two bottles of excellent wine, Bryan and Michelle shared the latest news headlines, celebrity gossip and scandals. Michelle promised to pass along her stash of British magazines to Nicole before they left the island, and Bryan offered to carry any letters they might like to send to friends and family.

By the time the dishes were washed and packed away for the return to Bryan's yacht and after-dinner drinks were poured, everyone was in a very mellow, congenial mood. Even Adam was telling jokes and treating Bryan and Michelle like old and dear friends.

Bryan sat on the sand, his back against a driftwood log, and balanced his drink on his upraised knee. "Since you've been on the island, have you learned any more about Passionata?" he asked, addressing Ian.

Ian, seated on the sand beside Nicole, shrugged. "Nothing beyond what's in the book you gave me. Adam's the history professor, not me."

Adam looked up from his position, half-reclined beside the fire. "There are all kinds of stories about Passionata," he said. "What do you want to know?

"The most scandalous tales, of course," Michelle said.

"Let's see...." Adam rubbed his chin, then said, "It's said the German Duke of Brunswick-Luneburg, who would later became Great Britain's King George, visited her once and asked her to teach him her secrets of seduction."

"Secrets of seduction?" Bryan asked.

"Yes," Adam said. "She had a reputation as a great seductress.

She and her female crew were said to be able to persuade sailors to abandon their duties in order to become the women's sexual slaves."

"Now that's an interesting idea," Michelle said, with a wicked grin.

"It is, isn't it?" Nicole agreed. If modern women like Michelle and her found the idea of turning the tables and putting women in charge of sexual encounters arousing, she could imagine how revolutionary and scandalous it must have been in Passionata's day.

"What happened to the duke?" Bryan asked. "Did Passionata teach him?"

Adam shook the ice in his glass. "The account I read said that the duke spent three days on the mysterious island and returned home a much-shaken man, who refused ever after to speak of his experiences there. He advised his country's sailors to 'steer well clear of the sorceress who inhabits there.'"

"Guess he couldn't handle it," Michelle said.

Nicole caught Ian's eye and exchanged a knowing look.

"I wonder what she did to the poor guy," Bryan said.

"If you've read her book, then you know Passionata contends that putting the woman in charge of the sexual relationship makes things better for both partners," Nicole said. "That a woman focused on ensuring her own satisfaction enjoys sex more, and thus her partner enjoys it more, as well."

"I can't think many men would put up with being pussy-whipped that way for long," Bryan said.

Ian shifted position and set his drink in the sand. "The men Passionata chose weren't the type to be cowed. Instead of beating them down, you might say she evened the stakes. Made them partners in their sexuality."

At his words Nicole thought of their encounters so far. There had been an equality there—the equality of each person focused on his/her own pleasure—both of them gaining equally from the encounter. She caught his eye and saw the desire she felt reflected there.

"So this Passionata was a good lay," Bryan said. "Was she any good at pirating?"

"She was one of the most successful buccaneers of her day," Adam said. "She captured dozens of ships from England, France and Spain, and recovered booty that would be worth millions in today's dollars."

"Now we're talking." Bryan rubbed his hands together. "Where's that treasure now?"

Adam studied Bryan through half-closed eyes. The others might have thought him bored, but Nicole knew Bryan's questions had aroused her friend's suspicions. "Why are you so interested?"

"Who wouldn't be interested in treasure?" Bryan asked. "I don't know about you, but I wouldn't mind finding a chest full of gold coins and jewels buried around here somewhere."

Adam shook his head. "There isn't any treasure."

"She must have done something with all that loot," Bryan persisted.

"She spent some, those of her crew who escaped took some with them, and the British claimed the rest," Adam said. "There's nothing left on this rock."

"I think the treasure is the island itself," Ian said. He stood and went around the circle, refilling glasses. "It's a true tropical paradise."

"Maybe if you're a bird or a clown fish," Bryan said. "And I can see the appeal for certain people, but it's too isolated for me."

"My idea of paradise is a five-star hotel with room service, a gold card with no limit and an endless supply of calorie-free, decadent chocolate," Michelle said.

"And where do I fit into that picture?" Bryan asked.

Michelle smiled at him. "I'll let you visit on alternate days."

"I guess the thing about paradise is it can only remain one if you just visit," Ian said. "I don't think it's someplace anyone could stand to live all the time. Even perfection can get old."

"No offense, but I don't think I even care to visit this place again," Michelle said. "There's something creepy about all these birds and the jungle and…" She shook her head. "Maybe I'm just in a weird mood, but it doesn't feel to me as if people have been happy here."

Bryan reached over and rubbed the back of her neck. "A fortune teller told Michelle once that she was sensitive, and she's taken that assessment to heart."

"She may be on to something, though." Adam sat up straight. "Passionata supposedly put a curse on the place. And it's true no one has managed to live here successfully since then."

"A curse!" Bryan laughed. "Hollywood couldn't have written a more fantastic story. In fact, I'm surprised no one's made a movie yet about the lady pirate who seduced sailors, acquired a fortune in treasure, then cursed those who came after her. It's brilliant."

"Do you think there's really such a thing as curses?" Michelle asked. "Maybe it's merely a psychological effect. People back then believed in curses, and that belief led to their own failure."

"I've heard the theory before," Adam said. "In 1842…"

While Adam expounded on the historical basis for curses, Nicole rose quietly and beckoned Ian to follow. He did so and when they were a short distance from camp, she wrapped her arms around him and kissed him. A long, languid kiss that telegraphed everything she wanted to do to him—and *with* him—without her saying a word.

9

WHEN NICOLE KISSED IAN, with the darkness wrapped around them like a cloak, it was as if the methodical, unassuming doctoral student had been replaced by a more primitive man. A man who relied not on reason but on instinct, who was ruled not by logic or intellect but by drive and desire. Lips locked to hers, he wrapped his arms around her and pressed her against the rough trunk of a coconut palm, one hand kneading her hip, the other braced beside her head against the tree.

He was seconds away from ripping the dress from her body and taking her right there—but loud laughter from the circle around the campfire brought him back to his senses and he reluctantly drew away.

She stared at him, lips parted, eyes lost in shadow. "Come with me," she whispered. "Come back to the boat with me."

She took his hand and he followed her down the trail and all the way to the beach. Only there, with the muffled thunder of waves crashing on the rocks as a background for their words, did they speak again. "Times like this, this really does feel like paradise," she said as they walked along the shore toward the anchored yacht.

"I supposed it is if you think of paradise as a place apart from the everyday world—a place where ordinary rules don't matter and we're free to indulge our fantasies."

She glanced at him. "That's what we're doing, isn't it? Indulging our fantasies. Sexual fantasies…and others, too. I mean, Adam's fantasy is to find a great treasure."

Ian nodded. He was indulging his own fantasy of being a man who truly experienced life instead of living in his head. "Tell me your fantasies," he said.

She was silent for a long moment. When they reached the beached Zodiac, she turned to him. "I think my fantasy, or at least the thing I want most, is to trust myself and my decisions again."

What role did he play in that fantasy? Was all this sexual experimentation an exercise to help her discover what she liked and didn't like—which decisions worked and which didn't? Or were they merely a temporary diversion?

With the tide in, they had to take the Zodiac to the yacht. They tied up the dinghy, then Ian followed her up the ladder and she pulled it up after them. "If Adam returns, when he sees the ladder in, he'll know not to disturb us."

"He won't be angry about being kicked off his own boat?"

She shrugged. "He might be a little annoyed, but all we'll need to do is distract him with talk of the treasure and he'll forget to be angry."

Ian laughed. "You know him pretty well, don't you?"

"Some men are easier to read than others."

He wondered if he fell into that category.

"Adam's a good guy, so his motives are always pretty clear," she added. "I can't say that for every man."

Was she referring to the doctor who dumped her—or to Ian himself?

She walked over to a pair of chaise lounges and dragged the cushions onto the deck. "Let's stay up here, where we can see the stars," she said. She lay down and beckoned him to lie beside her.

His earlier sense of urgency had fled, replaced with a lust that simmered below the surface, sharpening his senses and adding a pleasant edge to every moment. He stretched out beside Nicole, then rolled onto his side to face her.

She reached up and caressed his neck. "I liked what you said earlier, about Passionata's approach being to make the man and woman partners in their sexuality."

He smoothed his hand down her side, resting it in the dip of her waist. "That's how *I* see it, but I'm not so sure William D. or Passionata herself saw it that way."

"I think you're right," she said, as she slid her hand under his shirt and rested it on his stomach. She idly stroked her thumb back and forth, sending a tremor straight to his groin. "He saw his desire for Passionata as a weakness," she said. "She saw it that way, too, as a weakness to be exploited."

"Desire is a weakness only in the way that hunger and thirst are weaknesses." Ian inched closer to her, until they were thigh to thigh, torso to torso, aware of every soft curve and hard plane of each other's bodies. "It's a basic human drive."

"But sex isn't merely animal desire," she countered. "Emotion is involved, as well. I don't think even Passionata could separate that." She pushed her hand up higher, until it rested over his heart. "I haven't finished the book, but I think she started to care for William D."

He kissed her temple and the side of her cheek, inhaling deeply of her fragrance. "Do you think it's a female tendency to want every relationship to end in romance?"

"No." She tilted her head up to look into his eyes. "I think it's a human tendency to want to connect with another human being."

Her gaze was steady, unblinking, touching something inside of him, as if whatever artifice or mask he might ordinarily wear had been torn away. "I feel as if you and I have made a connection," he said.

"Yes," she breathed, and closed her eyes.

He kissed her, beginning tenderly, but the embrace soon turned fierce. She wrapped her leg over his and rolled him onto his back, straddling him as she had that first night in the hammock.

"Do you have something against the missionary position?" he asked, amused in the face of her intensity.

"I don't like the symbolism of it anymore," she said. She tilted her head forward, letting her hair fall around his face, tickling the side of his neck. "It forces the woman to be rather passive, don't you think?" she said.

He was having a hard time thinking of anything but the feel of her body atop his and the sweet scent of her surrounding him. "So you'd rather the man be passive?"

She smiled, a slow, seductive grin. "Maybe it's true what they say—power is an aphrodisiac. Even the little bit of power I have over you in this position." She emphasized the point by pushing down on his chest.

"I can't imagine you passive during sex." He had never been with a woman who had been more active and involved in each moment of their coupling.

"I was," she said. "You didn't know me then. Coming here to this island has liberated me." She grinned and began pulling his shorts down.

He wriggled out of the shorts, then shoved himself into a sitting position and removed his shirt, as well. He remained sitting, with her straddling his lap. "What about this?" he asked. "Face to face, as equals?"

She put her hands on his shoulders and squeezed, then trailed her fingers down his arms. "Yes. I think I might like this."

She squirmed, seating herself more firmly over him, and he realized there was nothing between him and her soft, moist center. "You're not wearing any underwear," he said.

Her smiled widened. "I was going to tell you sometime during dinner—just to give you something to think about—but I never got the opportunity."

Even in retrospect, the idea that she'd been sitting beside him all evening, naked from the waist down, was powerfully erotic. He reached up and tugged at the tie of the sarong. "I like this dress," he said. "Taking it off is like unwrapping a present."

She helped him unwind the length of fabric, then let the silky material puddle around them. He pulled her close and buried his nose in her neck, enjoying the feel of her snugged against him, desire building like a fire gathering intensity.

But Nicole could not be still for long. "I've wanted you all evening," she said, pulling away from his embrace. "I don't want to wait any more."

"I feel it, too," he said. "Why is it we can't get enough of each other?" He reached down and slid one finger into her tight, wet passage and reveled in the sharp intake of her breath and the way her eyes momentarily lost focus.

"I…I don't know." She panted and swallowed hard, fighting for control, even as she ground into him. "Is it some chemistry between us, or the strangeness of our circumstances? Being more or less stranded here for the summer."

Or did Passionata work some kind of magic so that her seductive presence was still felt? He discarded the idea as ridiculous and bent to suck the tip of one breast into his mouth. He pulled hard at it, her cry sending desire stabbing through him once more. She took hold of his erection, wrapping her fingers around him in a caress both tender and effective.

He tried to maintain control, to set a slower pace for their coupling, but Nicole's insistent hands and mouth, combined with his own raging lust, made it almost impossible to hold back. She pushed his hand away and opened her legs wide and guided him into her.

When she tightened around him, his vision fogged and a guttural cry rose from somewhere deep in his chest. She grew still, waiting, and when he could see clearly again she looked at him with a smile of triumph. So much for him thinking he would ever control her.

But the idea of her being out of control added more fuel to his desire, and he rocked forward, thrusting deeper.

She responded by drawing away, leaning back on her hands and establishing a rhythm of parry and thrust. He leaned forward and wrapped one arm around her, using the other hand to fondle her clit, remembering her complaint about men who expected her to climax without additional stimulation. As long as she was with him, he'd make sure she didn't have that problem.

Now that they were joined, their franticness faded, and they settled into a deliberate rhythm, sinking deeply, withdrawing, then coming together again. Waves of sensation shuddered through him, each more powerful than the last. He kept his eyes open, watching her face in the moonlight, marveling at the play of emotions there—need, anxiety, tension and, finally, joy reflected in a radiant smile.

He closed his own eyes then and abandoned himself to the need that gripped him. He took control of their dance now, thrusting harder and faster, rushing forward to meet the climax that welled up within him. His cry was an animal roar, a primitive shout of triumph.

They collapsed in each other's arms, limbs entwined, her cheek pressed against his shoulder, his chin resting atop her head. The smell of sex and salt and flowers was a sweet perfume surrounding them. Washed in moonlight, rocked gently by the waves that slapped against the side of the boat, Ian had never known such contentment.

Here in this brief moment of time, in this magical place, he had truly found paradise.

IAN LEFT THE YACHT a short time later. He took the Zodiac back to shore, then headed toward his camp. He heard voices and hid in the thick growth along the side of the path. Soon a flashlight beam played across the tree trunks and palm fronds, followed by Bryan, Michelle and Adam, who formed a crooked congo line snaking through the trees. They were laughing and singing a very off-key version of "Yes, we have no bananas," their faces flushed, happy in the way only the mildly inebriated can be.

Ian chuckled to himself as he watched them pass. Having his friends here had changed the whole character of the island. He loved seeing them, but they had brought a bit of the outside world with them—reminders of the life he'd led away from the island.

He wasn't ready to go back to that world yet, to surrender the fantasy that he was more than the studious doctoral student who was really nothing special. Here he was an explorer, an environmental crusader.

A skillful, amazing lover.

He didn't want to give up those things yet.

He wasn't ready to leave Nicole behind, either. Theirs wasn't the kind of relationship that survived in the real world. Jobs, newspaper headlines, bills, traffic and all the other details of real life interfered with the sex-swimming-lazing-on-the-beach-and-more-sex existence they currently enjoyed.

All he could do was hold on to the fantasy as long as possible and put off thinking about the day they'd say goodbye.

NICOLE THOUGHT OF THE next week as a kind of vacation from their vacation. Though Adam chafed at the delay in diving at the treasure site, she enjoyed entertaining Bryan and Michelle. The five friends snorkeled around the reef, braved the birds to explore Passionata's tower and spent a memorable day constructing an ingenious solar shower that made use of the plentiful cistern water and gravity to provide a luxurious shower bath that was a welcome change from washing her hair in a bucket on the deck of the yacht.

But at the end of the week, it was time for Bryan and Michelle to leave. They sailed away, bearing letters from the three remaining islanders to friends and family in England and the States, and a letter from Adam to a professor friend, in which he'd enclosed the gold coin he'd found in the fish. "Jefferson will verify the coin is from the right period to be part of the cargo on board the *Eve* and put some feelers out for me about funding a full-scale expedition," Adam explained to Nicole. "Meanwhile, we'll locate the wreck and the rest of the treasure."

Nicole, Adam and Ian loaded up their diving gear and headed out in Adam's Zodiac toward the spot where he'd caught the coin-laden fish. They planned to take turns diving, two going down while one remained on the Zodiac as backup. Adam had extra tanks, bags for retrieving small items and other specialized equipment, including Ian's underwater digital camera.

"What exactly are we looking for?" Nicole asked as she buckled on her weight belt.

"Anything out of the ordinary." Adam checked his air flow, then leaned over and checked Nicole's air flow. "Any irregularity on the bottom of the sea. It might look like a rock to you, but it could be part of the wreck, covered in coral."

"Or it could just be a rock," Ian said.

Adam ignored him. "I can't explain how, but I know when I

spot something that doesn't belong down there," he said. "I get a feeling in my gut. If you have questions about anything, motion me over and I'll check it out."

Adam and Nicole dove first. She slipped into the warm water with her usual apprehension, keeping an eye out for sharks.

She followed Adam toward the outermost edge of the reef, the sound of her own breathing echoing in her ears, a sound that always put her in a meditative mood. Where she had felt clumsy aboard the Zodiac in her flippers and the heavy diving tanks, here she felt buoyant and graceful.

Adam swam down, along the side of the reef, and she followed, marveling at the life teeming in every crevice of the bracketed coral. Colorful clown fish and butterfly fish swam among staghorn and brain coral. A slender blue and red fish darted into a crevice in the reef right in front of her. Ian probably knew the name of the fish. She wished he was the one diving with her instead of Adam.

In fact, with all his time occupied by Bryan and Michelle, she hadn't seen much of him lately. She'd have to arrange another private rendezvous for the two of them.

The idea made her laugh. Always before, she'd waited for the men in her life to set the schedule for their romance. Kenneth had explained very early in their acquaintance that because he had so many obligations and commitments, they would have to carefully schedule time to be together—at his convenience. Never mind if she'd planned to get together with friends on a night when he was free. She must cancel in order to be with him.

Not that she had minded at the time. She'd seen her willingness to change her schedule as an act of love. Only after they'd broken up had she realized the sacrifice had been all one-sided. In a relationship based on true love, both people would have compromised.

Or maybe that was a myth perpetuated in books, movies and music, she thought as she swam around the outermost edge of the reef. Maybe the reason she was so happy with Ian was that she didn't expect anything more from him than fun and great sex.

Yet where but a deserted island would she even attempt a relationship like theirs? She didn't want to think of the time when they'd leave the island and go their separate ways. But however sad she was to see him go, she knew she'd always be grateful to him for helping her to discover a side of herself she'd never had the courage to explore before. Never again would she put up with a man who thought he had to call all the shots.

That realization was the gift her time on the island—her time with Ian—had given her.

They crossed over the reef. Earlier, Adam had explained his plan to start at the reef and work outward, searching for any signs of the wreck. Nicole scanned the sea floor beneath her, looking for anything unusual. To a woman from Michigan, everything on the bottom of the ocean looked unusual. And she wasn't keen on reaching out to touch suspect rocks that might turn out to be hostile sea creatures or some passing yacht's discarded garbage.

For thirty minutes, they navigated around the reef. By the time they reached the far side, Nicole was beginning to feel chilled. She was about to swim up and try to get Adam's attention when he turned and pointed out something in the shadow of the reef.

Nicole swam beside him and stared in the direction Adam indicated. At first she saw nothing. Then something moved in the darkness beneath a coral shelf. A slender, slate-gray shape glided from the shadows, the tips of its fins edged in black. A shiver convulsed Nicole as she stared at the rows of pointed teeth in the slightly open slash of mouth on the underside of the long, tapered snout. Shark!

Heart pounding, she breathed heavily, bobbing up as her lungs filled with more air. She sent a panicked look at Adam, but he was calm, watching the shark swim away from them. She had heard that sharks were actually very nearsighted. This one likely hadn't even seen them. But she didn't like to take chances.

When the shark was out of sight, Adam started forward again. Nicole grabbed at his leg as he passed, managing to catch and hold a flipper. He looked back at her and she shook her head. No way was she heading in the same direction as that shark.

He looked exasperated and held up both hands, as if to indicate she had nothing to worry about. So she rubbed her shoulders to let him know she was cold and pointed toward the surface. It was time to go up top and take a break.

He nodded, but indicated he would stay down, flashing both hands to indicate ten minutes more. She wanted to object, but arguing with him would be a waste of air. He was an experienced diver, not one to take unnecessary chances. She held up her fingers to let him know she was holding him to the ten minutes, then headed toward the surface.

On the surface, Nicole pushed down her mask and searched for the Zodiac. As she bobbed in the waves, she didn't see it at first. But Ian must have been watching for her. He motored toward her, then throttled down and helped her back into the boat.

He aided her in removing her gear and handed her a bottle of water. "Did you find anything?

"No." She unzipped her wetsuit top, then took a long drink of water. "The wreck could be anywhere out there, if it hasn't broken up completely in the past three hundred years."

"Adam seems convinced he can find it."

She sat on the floor of the rubber dinghy, her back against the inflated sides. She could feel the waves slapping at the bottom of the craft. "I don't know what to look for down there. There aren't any helpful signs that say Shipwreck, This Way."

Ian smiled. "It's nice to think that even in these modern times, with all our technology, there are still discoveries that haven't been made."

"I certainly never knew about this place before Adam mentioned it," she said. "How did you find out about Passionata's Island?"

He hesitated. "A friend told me about it. It sounded interesting."

"Were you looking for an island where you could spend the summer, or did you decide that after you heard about the island?"

Again the hesitation, almost as if he didn't want to answer her question. He busied himself checking the regulator on his diving gear. "I decided after I heard about the island," he said finally.

"So you'd have peace and quiet to work on your book."

He nodded.

There was something he wasn't telling her. The idea gnawed at her. "Do you do this kind of thing often?" she asked.

"What kind of thing?"

"Go off by yourself for long periods of time? Are you a hermit at heart?"

He shook his head. "I wasn't planning on making this trip alone, remember?"

"That's right. Your girlfriend was going to come with you." Something tightened inside her chest at this acknowledgment that until recently he had been involved with—possibly in love with—another woman. Part of her resented that other woman, even though she knew it was illogical. But logic and emotion were two different countries that didn't speak the same language. "What was she like?"

"I don't want to talk about her. I'd rather talk about you." He knelt before her and kissed her, his hands grasping her shoulders.

She recognized this as an attempt to distract her but didn't object. He was a good kisser and maybe a distraction was exactly what she needed. She was torn between wanting to know more about Ian and feeling she has no right to ask. A certain amount of mystery in a man was sexy, but how much was too much? Why wouldn't he confide in her?

A muffled shout in the distance made them draw apart. She turned toward the sound and saw Adam bobbing on the surface a hundred yards away from them. He waved and shouted again, and Ian moved to the outboard motor. The Zodiac shot toward him, sweeping around him in a circle before idling near him.

Nicole and Ian helped him climb into the boat. "I think I've found something," he gasped as he fell between them.

"The wreck?" Nicole asked.

"Something big." He stripped out of his vest and tanks and tossed aside his mask, water streaming from his hair. "Definitely part of the shipwreck."

"What is it?" Ian asked.

Adam looked at each of them in turn, then grinned. "If it's what I think it is," he said. "It'll be worth a fortune."

10

ADAM'S EXCITEMENT WAS contagious, and Ian felt his adrenaline surge as visions of chests full of gold coins or caskets of jewels filled his head.

Nicole apparently shared these visions. She shoved Adam's shoulder. "Don't keep us in suspense," she said. "What did you find?"

"I think it's one of the ship's guns. Properly known as a demiculveren."

At their blank looks, Adam elaborated. "Like a cannon. Cast bronze, I'm sure," he said. "The one contemporary description of the *Eve* that I found describes it as carrying a demiculveren, two sakers and three minions—all types of small cannon."

Nicole's eyes met Ian's over the top of Adam's head as he droned on about "trunions" and "limbers" and "bores." She finally interrupted by punching Adam's shoulder again. "A cannon? That's your big treasure?"

His expression sobered and he stared at her a long moment. "Seventeenth-century armaments, especially with this kind of provenance, are priceless artifacts," he said. "Museums, not to mention collectors, would give a small fortune to own one."

Nicole's eyes met Ian's again. He read a spark of interest there now. She looked back at Adam. "So this cannon is worth a lot of money," she said. "But what about the real treasure? Do you think the rest of the ship is nearby? With the money and jewels?"

Adam nodded. "There's a shelf or valley in the ocean floor. It looks as if most of the wreck has slipped into that depression, but I could clearly see the keel bolts, part of an anchor chain and piles of cobblestones that would have been used for ballast."

"Congratulations!" Ian slapped the other man on the shoulder. "You did it. You've located the wreck of the *Eve*."

"I think it's the *Eve*. We won't know for sure until we can conduct a full-scale expedition. The best we can hope for now is to rescue a few artifacts." He rose to his knees. "For now, I want you to bring that camera of yours and come down with me."

"Wait just a minute," Nicole said. "You need to rest more first. Have some water and eat something."

Both men turned pained expressions to her. "Don't look at me like that," she snapped. "You know it's stupid to rush back down there and wear yourself out or risk getting hurt."

Ian knew she was right, but that didn't take away the frustration he felt at having to postpone seeing the object of their search.

Finally, after Adam had checked his regulators and cleaned his mask for the fifth time, Nicole agreed he'd rested enough. The two men donned their gear and headed down to the wreck.

Adam swam quickly underwater, with powerful strokes. Ian followed at a slower pace, orienting himself. The reef was on his right, relatively featureless ocean floor on the left. A stingray glided along the floor beneath him, fluttering gracefully across the sand.

His first impression of the object Adam pointed out to him was of a gray lump scarcely indistinguishable from the surrounding ocean floor. Then Adam swept his hand along what proved to be a long barrel. Ian began to make out the rough shape of a cannon.

He snapped photos from several angles, then Adam motioned him to follow. They swam roughly seventy-five yards, and the ocean floor dropped away beneath them, opening into a narrow canyon. Adam pointed at something projecting from the ocean floor—the unmistakable shape of a length of chain attached to an anchor.

Ian breathed hard, struck by the knowledge that he was looking at something that was quite probably more than three hundred years old. It had lain here on the ocean floor, undisturbed for three centuries. And he had helped discover it.

He took more pictures, and together he and Adam searched the ocean floor. Within minutes they'd discovered scraps of pottery, a metal flask and two more coins. These items they stashed in a bag tied to Adam's waist.

Finally, oxygen running low, they surfaced, both talking at once as they climbed back into the Zodiac.

"It's incredible…"

"Unbelievable."

"Wait till you see what else we found…."

"There must be hundreds of items."

"I can't believe…"

"Calm down," Nicole urged as she helped stash the heavy tanks in the center of the boat. When they'd stripped out of their wet suits and were seated, she faced them. "All right. Tell me what you've found."

"Look at this." Adam reached into the net bag and pulled out the tarnished flask.

Nicole took it, holding it between her thumb and forefinger. "This is from the wreck? No offense, but it looks like garbage."

"Look closer." Adam leaned in close and traced his finger around the neck of the flask. "There's engraving there. I'm pretty sure this is silver. Not the kind of thing a person would simply toss overboard." He grinned. "It might have belonged to Passionata herself."

Nicole hugged herself, as if to ward off a shiver. "It's unbelievable."

"There's more." Adam proudly showed off the fragments of pottery and two grime-encrusted coins. "They don't look like much now," he acknowledged. "But they should clean up nicely." He sat back on his heels. "Just think. We're looking at objects no human hands have touched in centuries."

They stared at the objects for a moment. On the surface, they did look like trash, but Ian had to admit there was an aura of age about the items that humbled him. "What do we do now?"

Adam replaced the items in the bag. "I'll try to clean up the flask and coins. We don't have the equipment or the time to bring up many larger items, but I'd like to get that demiculveren up."

Ian shook his head. The gun had been at least ten feet long. "It must weigh a ton."

"Almost two tons," Adam said. "Approximately thirty-six hundred pounds."

"How would we get something that heavy off the ocean floor?" Nicole asked.

"The way you raise anything out of the water," Adam said. "You make it float."

"What…with balloons?" Nicole asked.

Adam nodded. "Something like that. Take them down empty, attach them to the cannon, then inflate them and float them up."

"Do we have anything like that?" Ian asked.

"No," Adam admitted. "But I'll think of something."

Nicole stifled a yawn. "It's getting late. We should head back to the yacht."

The men agreed. The excitement and the physical work of diving had exhausted them all.

When they reached the yacht, Ian helped unload the Zodiac. It was agreed he'd leave his diving tanks and other gear on board the yacht to save him having to haul everything back and forth every day. When everything was secured, Adam retired to his cabin to research some way of salvaging the cannon in the dozens of books he'd brought with him, leaving Ian and Nicole on deck alone.

"I'd better get back to my camp," he said.

"Do you want me to come with you?" she asked.

He studied her, trying to read what she wanted to do, but her expression was indecipherable. "Do you want to?" he asked.

She smiled and stifled another yawn. "Let's say the spirit is willing…but the body is too tired."

He smiled. "Me, too." Then he kissed her. Not a passionate embrace, but a sweet one. The kiss of lovers who have a history and are confident of being with each other again. "Good night."

She stood on deck and waved to him when he reached the edge of the jungle. He thought how different leaving her was than leaving Danielle and other lovers he'd known. With them, every parting was accompanied by a certain anxiety and overanalysis. Did the fact that she didn't want to have sex with him mean her affection was waning? Did the ease with which he'd accepted the decision for them to spend the evening apart signal a change in his own feelings?

With Nicole, everything was so much easier. He'd see her again tomorrow. He was confident they'd have sex again, and that it would be a good experience. He could look forward to that encounter with pleasant anticipation. He didn't question her feelings or his feelings—Nicole was very special to him, but there was no pressure to analyze how special or what that meant for the future.

If anything, he avoided thinking about the future. On the island the only time that mattered was now. And right now he and Nicole had a satisfying bond that he had no inclination to break.

* * *

William D. rose from the bathtub, water streaming from his perfect, muscular form. I smiled to myself. Yes, I had chosen well.

"What happens now?" he asked. He reached for a towel and dried off but made no attempt to cover himself in my presence.

I stood in front of him and put my hands on his shoulders. Though I am a tall woman, he was taller still, and I had to reach up to grasp him. "Do you know how to pleasure a woman with your mouth?" I asked.

A sly smile formed on his lips. "Woman was made for the pleasure of man," he said.

I was tempted to chastise him for such insolence but reluctant to spoil my fun. Watching him in the bathtub had aroused me greatly, and I craved release. "A man who possesses the skills to please a woman sexually will find his own pleasure greatly enhanced."

I released him and turned away. "But if you are unwilling to learn, I will call the guard and send you back to your cell."

"No."

I smiled at the quickness of his answer, and waited, standing very still. I could see his reflection in the mirror across the wall—a big man, whose inward struggle was projected on his face. Pride warred against desire, but in the end, desire won. "What would you have me do?" he asked quietly.

I walked to my bed. It is an ornately carved piece, made especially for me by a sailor captured early in my reign on the island. He had a talent for woodworking, and fashioned this as a gift, in gratitude for all I had taught him and the good times we had shared.

This bed was very wide and long, with four posts that rose eight feet into the air. From the ceiling above was draped a great length of netting, dyed scarlet, which could be drawn around all sides of the bed, to shut out both biting insects and the world. On the finest rush-filled mattress are sheets of the most exquisite combed cotton from the South Seas, and blankets of quilted silk. Pillows of down cradle my head each night. It is a paradise of a bed, where all manner of fantasies may come true.

I drew back the covers of the bed, then turned to face William once more. "I am going to teach you," I said. "But you must do everything just as I ask. If you fail to obey, I will end it and send you away." I hoped I did not have to carry out this threat, but I meant it. A woman does not hold power by being indecisive or weak.

He started toward me, then stopped. "May I approach?" he asked. His expression was humble, but there was laughter in his eyes.

My heart pounded faster at the sight. I appreciated a man who saw the playful nature of the sexual encounter. It boded well for our future.

"Yes, you may approach," I said, allowing my expression to betray none of my tender feelings toward him.

When he was standing in front of me, I put my hands on his shoulders and looked into his eyes. "You may touch me," I said.

It was the first time I had invited him to touch me with his hands. He reached out to caress my shoulders and I noticed the faint tremor in his hand. The sight moved me, and my womb contracted with anticipation.

His hand was big and warm, calluses dragging against my skin as he stroked my shoulder and arm. "You are beautiful," he breathed, and threaded a lock of my hair between his fingers.

"I am the woman of your fantasies," I said.

He nodded, and his eyes met mine. Intense. Truly wanting to pleasure me and thus to find pleasure for himself, as well.

My hands still on his shoulders, I moved backward, climbing into bed. I knelt before him, and released my hold on him. Then I cupped my breasts and offered them to him. "Taste me."

He latched on to my breast with the eagerness of a hungry infant and began to suckle. I laughed and pushed him back. "I am your lover, not your wet nurse," I scolded.

A hot blush swept up his face. His vulnerability touched me, and I gentled my words. "Imagine that your tongue is a brush with which you will paint a masterpiece," I said. "And my breasts are the canvas for your art."

He moved to my breasts again, too gentle at first, then as he swept his tongue back and forth across the tip and I pushed toward him, he became inspired. He traced circles and ripples across my skin, painting landscapes of waves and clouds, moving away from that most sensitive peak, then drawing to it once more.

"Take me into your mouth," I instructed. "As much of me as you can."

He did as I asked, then rubbed the flat of his tongue back and forth across my nipple, sending exquisite sensations through me. I could not keep back a moan, and I felt him smile against me. He grasped my hips and pulled me closer, and turned his attention to my other breast.

I was trembling all over by the time I found the strength to push him away. He frowned. "Don't tell me you weren't enjoying that," he said.

"I was enjoying it," I said. "But you have more to learn." I lay back on the bed and motioned for him to lie beside me. He lay on his side, his erection pressed against my thigh, the heat of it burning into me.

I took his hand and dragged it down between my thighs. "There is a magic button here," I said, "that, when touched, brings a woman great pleasure."

He smiled, and parted my nether lips to find this button. "I am not ignorant," he said, and proved this by fondling this center of my arousal.

I grasped his wrist to still him before he robbed me of the powers of speech altogether. "I see you possess certain skills," I said. "Did you know also that if you stroke this button with your tongue—as you have just stroked my breasts—it can bring the greatest pleasure of all?"

His eyebrows drew together in a frown. I could see he was unsure of this idea. I leaned closer and kissed his cheek. "Have you ever had a woman take your shaft in her mouth?"

He grunted, then nodded.

"And did you enjoy it?"

He nodded again and licked his lips. "Are you going to do that now?" he asked. I could feel his shaft thrusting against me, like an impatient child demanding sweets.

I laughed. "No. You are going to do it to me."

I pushed him downward. He hesitated, then slid lower. I slipped my legs over his shoulders, my back against a pile of pillows so that I could watch. Seeing things happen can be part of the pleasure.

He was tentative at first, unsure of himself. I pressed myself more firmly against his mouth. "Pretend you're licking a fruit ice," I said. "The best fruit ice you've ever tasted."

He responded with a firmer pressure then, long sweeps of his tongue that sent jolts of sensation through me. "That's it," I urged. "You don't want to miss a drop."

He grasped my thighs and spread them wider, allowing him better access. I trembled against him, unable to control myself. "Do you see how aroused this is making me?"

"Yes." His voice was muffled.

"Does it make you hard, knowing you've put me in this state?"

"Yes!" As if to emphasize this, he thrust his tongue inside my passage. I leaned my head against the pillows and let out a moan.

He was an apt pupil, not afraid to experiment. He varied the pressure and the length of his strokes. He licked and suckled while I fought to hold back my release. I wanted to draw out the pleasure as long as possible.

But this man who had professed such reluctance at first proved talented indeed, and before long my defeat was inevitable. I closed my eyes and surrendered to the sweet waves that lifted me to new heights of pleasure.

My body was still pulsing when he rose on his hands and knees and loomed over me. I opened my eyes to meet his, and he covered my mouth with his. I tasted my own juices as he thrust into me, filling me completely.

It was a coupling unlike any I had ever known, a joining of both body and spirit. We danced in perfect rhythm, my hips rising up to meet each thrust, my fingers playing along the perfection of his shoulders and back, caressing and stroking, reveling in his strength. His very *maleness*.

His climax was fierce, and as he spilled his seed in me I joined him in exultation. This is what intimate consort should be, this meeting of equals face-to-face, each desiring both to pleasure and be pleasured. A woman who accepts less is denying both herself and her lover the most exquisite of sensations.

When he withdrew from me, we lay side by side among the pillows, silent, though still touching, as if reluctant to relinquish contact. After a while, I thought he was sleeping, but when I made to leave the bed, he reached for me. "If I stay here with you, will you teach me more?"

"I will, but you must be a good student," I said, making my expression severe. "If you are not, I will punish you." I emphasized my point with a hard slap across his naked backside.

He laughed and grinned. "I have a feeling you could make me find pleasure even in a whipping."

I rubbed my hand across the flesh I had just chastised, the first shiver of reawakening desire coursing through me. "Perhaps we will experiment sometime."

"I am eager to learn from you."

"We will teach each other," I reassured him. "For the teacher may always learn from the student."

He smiled, and the expression transformed his face to true handsomeness. "I never looked forward to lessons so much as I anticipate these. But then—" and at this he pulled me into his arms "—never did I have such a teacher."

And never had I such a student.

11

THE NEXT MORNING ADAM announced that he'd come up with a way to raise the cannon. They'd use the yacht's rubber life raft and inflate it with the air compressor once they'd fastened the cannon to it. "A raft is just a big flotation device," he said. "We'll weight it to get it down to the bottom,."

But this wasn't as easy as it sounded. Getting a large, awkward, rubber object designed to float down to the site of the wreck took a great deal of maneuvering and occupied them for most of one day. The next day, getting the cannon onto the raft without puncturing it proved to be the next problem. Initially, Adam had planned to roll the cannon into the center of the uninflated raft, but having sat on the ocean floor for almost three centuries, the weighty bronze gun was not inclined to move.

"That's all right," he said when they returned to the Zodiac at the end of this frustrating day to reconsider the situation. "We'll lash the demiculveren to the underside of the raft. When we inflate it, the raft will do the work of raising the gun toward the surface."

But this proved problematic as well. The cannon was covered in sharp barnacles and corrosion, and the risk of puncturing even the thick rubber of the raft was very real. Then there was the question of what to use to secure the gun to the raft. What material would prove flexible enough, yet strong enough to bear the weight?

After two days of experimentation, they settled on placing a canvas tarp between the gun and the bottom of the raft for cushioning. Then they dismantled part of the yacht's rigging and used the rope to fasten the gun in place.

While they worked, they were shadowed from time to time by one or more black-tipped sharks. The sinister creatures kept their distance and the men ignored them. "They're probably just curious about the noise or what we're doing down here," Adam said. But he kept a spear gun near by just in case.

Still, Nicole refused to stay down when the sharks were anywhere in sight, and tried to convince the men to do the same. "You worry too much," Adam told her, and continued to work on raising the cannon, to the point of exhaustion.

While the men worked, Nicole spent her time either waiting in the Zodiac or gathering smaller artifacts and cataloging them. Adam had drawn a map of the area around the wreck, on which she plotted the location of each find, also photographing the item before removing it from the ocean floor.

So far she had found nothing spectacular—more broken pottery, a bent spoon, a man's carved pipe and several cast-iron cannon balls. "Where are the jewels and money and things like that?" she asked one afternoon when they broke for lunch.

"Probably most of it's buried under the remains of the ship," Adam said.

"Let's dive over there this afternoon," she said. "I want to see."

"I was hoping to try inflating the raft today," Adam said.

"You can do that tomorrow," she said. "What's one more day when you've been working a week already?" She leaned toward him, her tone wheedling. "Besides, aren't you curious to know what's there?"

He blew out a breath, then nodded. "All right. But everyone be very careful. These old wrecks can be unstable."

Her stomach flip-flopping with excitement, Nicole led the way toward the wreck site. As they swam into the chasm, the water temperature dropped and she felt cold. But it wasn't just the temperature change that made her shiver. The remains of the ship below had an eerie quality. At first she saw nothing but piles of rubble, but as she looked closer, she began to distinguish what was left of the ship—a trio of cannon balls amidst a pile of barrel hoops, an iron stanchion that had once anchored a mast, a coil of anchor chain. The wood had long since rotted away, leaving rusting keel bolts jutting up like skeletal fingers.

Thinking of skeletons, Nicole swallowed hard. People had died in this shipwreck. She didn't like to think of suddenly swimming up on their bones.

She followed Adam and Ian toward the wreckage. Adam motioned toward the left and she turned to see the toothy, pointed snout of a barracuda peeking out from behind a pile of ballast. She nodded to show she'd gotten the message. Barracudas weren't as vicious as sharks, but they would attack if provoked, and those teeth looked as if they could do some damage.

They swam over the site, Ian taking pictures of iron bolts, sea urchin–covered ballast stones and the ship's anchor. Nicole stared at the massive anchor, easily six feet across, and imagined Passionata standing on the deck of the *Eve,* in command of her crew. The sailors who worked for her were said to be mostly women, though Nicole wondered if some seamen hadn't chosen to throw in their lot with the pirate queen.

Had William D. been there, as well? Had he and Passionata taken their sexual lessons to sea?

The idea made her smile, and distracted her from keeping a close eye on her companions. Adam hovered over a pile of what looked like wine bottles. Many of them were shattered, but he searched and found one that was intact.

Ian, meanwhile, had drifted toward a jumble of barrel hoops and rusted metal. He tried to separate one of the hoops and his line snagged on the jagged metal.

Nicole realized what was happening and swam over to Adam and directed his attention to Ian. Together they were able to free their colleague. They hovered together, varying degrees of fear reflected on all their faces. Adam pointed toward the surface and Ian and Nicole nodded.

They returned to the Zodiac and no one said anything until they had removed their gear. Adam examined the line between Ian's air tank and pressure gauge. It had been pinched, not severed, but it would need to be replaced. "Funny how such a little thing can shake you up," Ian said, looking at the line.

"It's not funny at all," Adam said. "It's why diving wrecks is dangerous."

"I won't go back there again." Nicole hugged her arms tightly around her body. "It's creepy down there."

"We won't go back," Adam agreed. "We'll save that for a properly outfitted salvage expedition."

"It seems…almost wrong somehow, to disturb the place," Nicole said. "I mean, people died there. It's almost like looting a graveyard."

"It's nothing like that at all," Adam said. "Whoever died there has been gone three hundred years. All we're doing is saving valuable artifacts from further decay and preserving an important part of history."

"Yes, professor," she said.

"I don't mean to lecture," he said. "But people don't understand how important this work is."

Nicole didn't understand, but what did it matter? This was Adam's pet project. She was here to help him.

THE MORNING AFTER HIS close call aboard the *Eve*, Ian and Adam made their first attempt at raising the demiculveren. In addition to the raft, Adam had decided to add two empty cylinders that had held compressed air. He lashed these to either side of the gun's barrel.

With Nicole up top, keeping an eye on the compressor and the line stretching from it to the salvage operation, Adam filled the air canisters, then began inflating the raft. It was a big one, designed to hold four people.

The sharks were back this morning—two of them, their sleek gray sides blending with the shadows. The cold eyes and rows of sharp teeth were enough to unsettle anyone, but Adam scarcely seemed to notice.

And he was right that sharks seldom attacked people. These two certainly appeared nonaggressive. They were merely curious about the commotion these two intruders were making in their home.

As the air hissed into the canisters, nothing happened. Adam switched to the raft and it was a while before Ian noticed any change. But as he shifted position against the gun, he felt it rock slightly. He gave a thumb's-up sign to Adam, who nodded and kept working.

Then, magically, the cannon lifted off the ocean floor slightly before settling once more. Adam motioned they should help it along, so the two men braced their shoulders to the gun and shoved upward.

The movement was awkward underwater. When Ian took a deep breath, preparing to put more effort into his movements, he bobbed up and lost his grip on the gun. But finally they heaved together and the cannon rose, slowly. The raft did, indeed, act much like a balloon, lifting the gun upward.

With a man on either side, they were able to guide the awkward craft toward the surface.

When the raft broke through to float on the surface, the gun suspended beneath swung around wildly, clipping Ian's shoulder. Pain shot through him and he fell backward in the water before regaining his composure. Arm throbbing, he swam upward once more and took his position on one side of the raft. Propelling themselves forward with strong kicks, he and Adam began steering their ungainly craft toward the Zodiac.

The plan was to secure the raft to the Zodiac then tow the cannon to shallow water. Once there, Adam thought they could winch it onto shore.

With the bulk of the raft and cannon between them, the two men couldn't see each other. But as the two of them guided the raft slowly through the water, Ian felt a violent tug on the line. He looked around to see what had happened and heard a muffled cry. He released his hold on the raft and swam around toward Adam.

As he rounded the raft he was astounded to see the professor clutching his leg, his face contorted in pain. A movement out of the corner of his eye caught Ian's attention and he turned to see one of the sharks circling around to make a second pass.

Ian's stomach lurched, and before he realized what he was doing, he had his belt knife in his hand. Meanwhile, Adam had unshouldered the spear gun and fired at his attacker.

The gun missed, but was enough to frighten off both sharks— at least momentarily.

Ian grabbed the gun away. Adam tried to fight him, but Ian motioned to the blood swirling from the gash on Adam's thigh.

Not only was the other man losing an alarming amount of blood, but also the smell of it was sure to attract the sharks...and their friends.

He shoved Adam onto the raft. The injured man had to literally pull himself up the ropes that held the cannon, but with Ian's help he managed. He was very pale now, shock setting in.

Keeping a wary eye out for the sharks, Ian hauled himself up after Adam and signaled for Nicole.

She'd already spotted them and motored the Zodiac alongside. The two men fell into the craft.

"What happened?" she cried, kneeling beside them.

"Shark." Ian grabbed a towel and used it as a tourniquet around Adam's bleeding thigh. "We need to get him back to the yacht before he loses any more blood."

"The cannon!" Adam cried.

"We can come back for it later," Ian said.

"No." Adam shook his head and motioned toward the raft bobbing behind them. "It won't take a minute to fasten the lines."

"I'll look after him while you do that," Nicole said.

Arguing would waste precious time, so, cursing Adam's stubbornness, Ian did as she asked. He used a gaff to grab the trailing lines and tie them fast to the back of the Zodiac.

As he did so, two ominous shadows were visible on the right side of the boat.

"Let's get the hell out of here," he said, moving over to the Zodiac's motor.

It wasn't possible to make much speed towing the cannon, but he kept a steady pace, heading not for Adam's yacht, but for his camp, which was closer. "I've got first aid supplies," he shouted to Nicole above the roar of the motor and wind. "You can stitch him up there."

She nodded, using bottled water and cotton wool to clean the jagged wound, which continued to seep blood. Adam watched her, his mouth a tight line, eyes dark against his pale skin.

Ian ran the Zodiac right onto the shore and leaped onto the sand as soon as he'd cut the engine. Nicole helped Adam over the side, then Ian hooked his shoulder under the other man's arm and half carried him to the camp.

"Put him in the shade over there and bring me your first-aid supplies," Nicole said. "I'll need sutures and disinfectant." She turned to her patient. "When was the last time you had a tetanus vaccination?"

"Right before we left on this trip," he said.

She knelt beside him, carefully probing the wound. "It's deep, but it doesn't look as if there are any major blood vessels severed."

Ian brought her the ammo box that held his supplies. She took out a bottle of antiseptic and poured it over her hands, then over Adam's thigh.

He shouted a curse and glared at her. "What are you trying to do—torture me?"

She ignored him and continued to clean the wound, then dried it carefully. Selecting a packet of suture silk and a long curved needle, she sat back on her heels and took a deep breath. "This is going to hurt, but I don't suppose it will be much more uncomfortable than you already are."

Without being asked, Ian went to the locker where he kept his more perishable supplies and took out a bottle of scotch—a parting gift from Bryan and Michelle. "Here," he said, and thrust it at Adam.

Adam sent him a grateful look and unscrewed the cap. He made a face as he took a long swallow, then coughed. "Be better with ice and soda," he said.

"Sorry I couldn't accommodate you."

Then they all fell silent as Nicole began stitching,

Ian watched her, impressed by her serenity. She might have been sewing a sampler, her attention focused on making neat stitches with even knots. When she was done, the gash was effectively closed, swelling only slightly. She slathered on antibiotic ointment and nodded. "I've got antibiotic capsules back at the yacht. I think you should take them for a few days to ward off infection."

"How soon can I dive again?" Adam asked.

She stared at him. "Not until that heals. A couple of weeks at least."

"I haven't got that long," he said. "I'll wear the full wet suit."

"No you won't." Her voice was hard, truly angry now. "You'll stay in the Zodiac and tell Ian and me what to do."

"Don't be ridiculous. I'll be fine."

She put her hand on Adam's arm, squeezing hard. "Don't be stupid," she said. "We can't take foolish chances out here. We're two hundred miles from the nearest hospital. If you develop sepsis or staph or any of a dozen other nasty infections you could be dead before help arrived."

This outburst sobered him. He sat back. "All right."

She looked at Ian. "Can you help me get him back to the ship?"

"Of course."

They decided to load Adam into Ian's Zodiac to transport him back to the yacht. "What about the demiculveren?" Adam asked as they helped him to his feet.

"It will be fine where it is for now," Ian said. "I'll go out this afternoon and make sure it's anchored properly."

Nicole gave Adam some pain meds, then, braced between them, he hobbled toward Ian's Zodiac. "How are we going to get him aboard the yacht?" Nicole asked as the three of them collapsed into the raft. "We'll never get him up the ladder in this condition."

"Why don't we make a camp for him on the beach?" Ian seated himself in the bow and began guiding the Zodiac out of the lagoon. "He can sleep in the hammock." The same hammock where he and Nicole had first had sex.

By the time they reached the beach near the yacht, the pain meds were starting to take effect and Adam could scarcely walk. The three of them staggered to the hammock and managed to get Adam into it. "Why didn't we leave him at your camp?" Nicole asked.

"I'm sorry I didn't think of it," Ian said, feeling foolish. In the weeks they'd been on the island together, he'd come to think of the small expanse of land in terms of his side versus Adam and Nicole's side.

"It doesn't matter now," she said. "And he's probably better off here where I can keep an eye on him. I'll bring some pillows and things to make him more comfortable."

"I'll be fine," Adam said groggily. He was pale and looked utterly exhausted. He'd lost a lot of blood. Ian imagined it would be a few days before he was feeling like himself again.

"The pain meds should help you sleep," Nicole said. She patted his arm and checked the stitching on his thigh, which still looked smooth and even. "I'll bring you the antibiotics and some water."

She and Ian took the Zodiac to the yacht. He followed her up the ladder and waited while she rummaged in the small galley. "What happened down there?" she asked.

"I didn't see the attack, but apparently while we were distracted moving the gun, one of the black-tips that's been following us around all week moved in and attacked."

She shuddered. "Thank God you reacted so quickly. You probably saved his life. Or at least his leg."

"Is he going to be all right?"

She nodded. "He should be. It's a clean wound and I didn't see any serious damage. He's lucky."

"We saw the sharks earlier," Ian said. "We should have left then."

"That's Adam." She filled a waterproof pouch with supplies and slung it over her shoulder. "I told you he was single-minded. He'd have never listened to you."

Still, Ian felt guilty. He'd been as focused and oblivious to everything else as Adam had been. "I'll come back this afternoon to check on you both," he said when he and Nicole reached the beach once more.

"Please stay." She put her hand on his arm. "I don't want to be alone. Adam will sleep for a while now."

In fact, Adam was already asleep when they returned to the beach. Nicole left the antibiotic tablets in an Altoids box, alongside a glass of water on a stump drawn up beside the hammock to serve as a bedside table. Then she and Ian walked down the beach, out of sight, but within earshot of their patient.

"It's too hot to stand around out here," Nicole said. "Let's go in the water."

Before Ian could respond, she undid the top of her bikini and let it fall. He stared as the bottom followed and she stood before him, naked in the bright sun, her breasts pale against her golden tan. He had always found tan lines erotic, as if the whiteness of certain body parts emphasized their private and forbidden nature.

"Aren't you going to join me?" she asked, staring pointedly at his swim trunks, the fly of which was already beginning to tent with his growing erection.

He stripped off his trunks and left them on the sand with her swimsuit, and together they walked into the water. Here in the lagoon, it was calm and clear, protected from the rougher waves. He dove under, enjoying the refreshing feel of the sea on his skin.

Nicole swam past, brushing against him, moving gracefully, sleek as a seal. He swam after her, but she was agile and evaded him. They rose to the surface and burst through in a shower of spray, laughing. She splashed him and he splashed back, slapping the water hard. She ducked and dodged, sweeping her opened palm across the surface of the water to drench him.

He lunged and caught her, and held her while she squirmed against him. "I've got you now," he said. "I won't let go."

She ceased struggling. "Then don't," she said. "Don't let go." She wrapped her arms around him and all the energy seemed to rush out of her. When her eyes met his, he was stunned at the sadness he saw there. "What's wrong?" he asked, stroking one finger down her cheek.

"When I saw Adam bleeding, I was so scared," she whispered, and pressed her face against his shoulder.

He held her tightly, trying to contain her trembling. "You were great," he said. "You took good care of him. He'll be fine."

"I know." She raised her head and looked at him again. "I can be good in a crisis, but afterward, I fall apart."

He nodded. "The adrenaline leaves and you get the shakes," he said. "It happens to me, too."

"I feel better here with you." She closed her eyes and tilted her head toward him in silent invitation.

The kiss was long and deep, a kiss he hoped would drive away all fear and bad thoughts. As their tongues entwined, she relaxed against him, her breasts cool against his chest, her thighs firm against his own. She wrapped her legs around him, rubbing against his erection. The combination of hot sun, warm water and naked flesh heightened his arousal and added to the feeling that this was yet another moment of fantasy fulfilled.

She put her hands on his shoulders and settled herself more tightly against him. He was beginning to think they should move to the beach when—*bllaaaattt*.

Heart pounding, he raised his head as the blare of the air horn resounded around them.

"What the hell?" Nicole asked.

Still clinging to each other, they stared out to sea, the direction the horn had sounded from, and saw a sleek cabin cruiser motoring into the bay.

A stunning brunette in a red bikini waved to them from the deck. She wore binoculars around her neck and carried a bullhorn. "Hello, there," she called, apparently unperturbed to find two naked people standing in the shallows of a reputedly deserted island. "Sorry to interrupt. Are you the treasure hunters?"

12

NICOLE STARED AT THE woman, with her Hollywood smile and gleaming white yacht and her preposterous query about treasure hunters. "Tell me I'm not hallucinating," she whispered to Ian.

"You're not hallucinating," he said. "Unless I am, too."

"And we didn't, like, eat any funny mushrooms or anything, did we?"

"No mushrooms." He shook his head. "I'm afraid this is real."

"That's what I thought. So who the hell is that and what is she doing here? And how does she know about the treasure?"

"I don't know the answer to any of that," he said. "But I do know that at some point we're going to have to get out of the water, and our clothes are a long way away." He looked toward the beach, where the small pile of fabric that constituted their swimsuits lay.

"Let's pretend she's not there," Nicole said.

He looked toward the yacht, which was clearly twice as large as Adam's boat. "How can we ignore that?" he asked.

"We just will." If she could keep operating on the principle that this was a crazy fantasy or dream, she could walk out of here without a second glance.

She slipped her arms and legs from around Ian, turned and walked toward the shore. She refused to look back or hurry, as if she just happened to be taking a leisurely stroll to the shore.

She made it to the patch of sand where they'd left their clothes and bent to pick up her swimsuit bottoms.

At that moment, the air horn blared again, and the brunette's voice sounded over the bullhorn, "I hope you don't mind that we're filming this."

Holding the swimsuit in front of her, Nicole whirled and glared at the other woman. Sure enough, a man with a handheld video camera stood beside her. The brunette waved cheerily.

Fuming, Nicole turned her back, dressed, then marched toward the yacht.

Ian soon caught up with her. "We'd better warn Adam we've got company," he said.

She stopped. "Oh my gosh, I forgot about Adam." She turned and ran toward the hammock.

When Nicole and Ian leaned over him, Adam blinked up at her. "Did I hear a boat horn?" he asked. "Or was I dreaming?"

"It was a boat horn," Ian said. "We've got company."

"More friends of yours?" Adam asked.

Ian shook his head. "I've never seen them before."

Adam struggled to sit. He squinted out toward the lagoon. The yacht was visible, anchored some distance from shore. "Sweet ship," he said.

"The first thing the woman on board asked when she hailed us was if we were the treasure hunters," Ian said.

Adam blinked. "She said *the* treasure hunters? Not just generic treasure hunters?"

"I'm pretty sure she said *the*." Ian looked at Nicole.

She nodded in confirmation. "I don't know what she's doing here, but I wish she'd leave," she said.

Adam raised one eyebrow. "Do I sense a little hostility? You don't even know this woman."

"I don't have to know her to know I don't like her." Nicole

didn't waste her breath trying to explain. It wasn't only that the brunette had filmed Nicole naked, or the fact that she stood in the prow of that huge yacht like a conquering queen, or that she seemed so amused to have caught Ian and Nicole in flagrante delicto. It was also an intangible female instinct that told Nicole their visitor was up to no good.

Worse, the arrival of this intruder was a harsh reminder of the outside world they'd all have to return to soon, which would mean the end of their island fantasy and her affair with Ian.

She shook her head to drive out the depressing thoughts and checked Adam's thigh. The wound was a little pink, but otherwise in great shape. "How do you feel?" she asked.

"Fine, thanks to those magic pills of yours." He swung his legs over the side of the hammock and eased into a standing position, wincing as he put his full weight on the injured leg.

"You should stay off your feet for a while longer," she said.

He shook his head. "The sooner I'm moving around, the better." He turned to Ian. "You have to hide the demiculveren from these newcomers."

Ian nodded. "I can pull the raft into a bog near my camp and camouflage it with branches."

"Do it."

"Then what are you going to do?" Nicole asked.

Adam smiled. "Then we're going to welcome our visitors."

"And if they ask about the treasure?" she asked.

He assumed a blank expression. "What treasure? I don't have any idea what you're talking about."

THE BRUNETTE DIDN'T WAIT long to pay them a visit. Ian was scarcely out of sight before a trim motorboat raced into the lagoon. A smiling, tanned sailor helped her into the water and she tripped gracefully over to join them.

"Hello, I'm Sandra Newman." She offered her hand.

Nicole had trouble keeping her mouth from dropping open. Now that she'd gotten a good look at their visitor, she recognized her as a television personality known for her ratings-busting documentaries. Sandra Newman had talked her way into unrestricted access to pro baseball locker rooms during a steroid scandal. She'd been the first to reveal an eastern state's governor's affair with his male secretary. One of her most popular shows had given viewers a peek at the private art collections of some of the wealthiest people in the United States.

If Adam recognized the name, he gave no sign of it. He shook her hand but didn't offer his name. "What brings you to Passionata's Island?" he asked.

Her smile broadened and she moved even closer. Though she wasn't a large woman—except for her impressive bustline—she had a dominating personality. In fact, Sandra was as larger-than-life as the stories she covered. "Am I speaking with Professor Adam Carroway, of the University of Michigan?"

Adam's eyes widened, and for a moment he allowed his surprise to show. "How do you know my name?"

"I read your bio on the University Web site." She lowered her voice to a confidential tone. "I must say, your photograph there doesn't do you justice."

Adam was unmoved by this attempt at flattery. "What are you doing here?"

She straightened, all business once more. "I'm here to film a documentary about your discovery of pirate's treasure."

Adam's expression remained impassive. "You must have the wrong island. I don't know anything about any treasure." He made a show of looking around them. "There's nothing on this island but palm trees and a lot of noisy birds."

Sandra's smile never faltered. "Then how do you explain the

picture I have of a seventeenth-century gold sovereign you reportedly found off the coast of this very island?"

Adam's mouth tightened. "What makes you think I found a coin like that?"

"I also have a copy of the letter that accompanied the coin, in which you describe the find as 'possibly one of the richest treasures to be discovered since the recovery of the Spanish galleon, *Nuestra Señora de Atocha* in 1985.'" She paused as if to gauge how well he was taking this revelation. "The *Nuestra Señora,* I'm sure you recall, yielded a treasure valued at four hundred million dollars."

Adam's face reddened. "How did you get hold of that letter?" he asked, abandoning his pretense of ignorance.

"I have a friend who works for the university," she said. "She saw the letter and the coin and knew I'd be interested."

He took a step toward her, fists clenched at his side. "I'm sorry you've wasted your time, traveling all this way. I'm not interested in a documentary."

"Then I'll make the film without your cooperation. In fact, Damian has been filming this conversation." She gestured behind her, to the sailor who had brought her over. He did, indeed, have a video camera aimed at them.

Nicole was sure Adam was ready to attack the man—an attack that would be filmed and no doubt be a highlight of the planned documentary. She latched on to his arm. "I think we'll head back to our boat now," she said. "I'm sure Ms. Newman is smart enough to figure out fairly quickly that there's nothing worth filming on this island."

"Where's the other man that was here?" Sandra turned to Nicole. "The one you were frolicking with when we arrived."

"Frolicking?" Nicole stared at her.

"I could be more crude. Would you prefer I said the man you were f—"

"He went back to his own camp," Nicole said. Though she was sure Adam suspected she and Ian were more than platonic friends, she preferred to keep the extent of their relationship private.

"Maybe I can persuade *him* to tell me about the treasure," Sandra said.

Adam grunted, and started limping toward the yacht.

Sandra followed. "Why are you limping?" she asked.

Adam didn't answer.

Sandra put out a hand, stopping him, and bent to examine the row of stitches on his thigh. "Very nice work." She looked at Nicole. "Did you do this?"

Nicole hesitated, then nodded. "I'm a nurse."

But Sandra was focused on Adam once more. "That looks like it must have hurt," she said. "What happened?"

When he didn't answer, she continued, undaunted. "Did it happen while you were diving? Perhaps you injured yourself on the shipwreck itself. Or maybe you're just clumsy."

"It was a shark," he said. "And I wasn't anywhere near the wreck when it happened."

"That's right," Nicole gave Sandra a condescending smile. "I'd be careful doing any diving around here. The sharks are vicious."

Maybe Nicole imagined that Sandra turned paler under her tan, but the reporter scarcely missed a beat. "I don't have to dive," she said. "I have people to do that for me."

Adam limped away.

"Let me come up to your boat and we'll discuss this more," Sandra said.

"No."

Sandra turned to Nicole. "What is his problem? I'm prepared to make him famous."

"Not everyone wants fame," Nicole said. "But then, I guess you wouldn't understand that."

With this parting shot, she hurried after Adam. She was under no illusion that the other woman would give up her quest to film the treasure. She'd have her minions turning the island upside down, searching for clues to its location, and she'd be watching every move Adam or Nicole made.

And before too long, she was bound to meet Ian. The thought of Sandra's powerful personality and impressive boobs meeting up with the handsome Englishman made Nicole's stomach hurt. Sure, Nicole had no real claim on the man, but right now he was *her* lover. What woman wouldn't be upset at the prospect of someone else poaching on her territory?

IAN SPENT THE REST of the afternoon cutting palm fronds to hide the demiculveren and the bright-yellow life raft. It was hot, sweaty work. By the time he finished, he wanted nothing more than a shower and a stiff drink, but he was anxious to get back to the other side of the island and learn more about their latest visitor. So he settled for a quick swim in the ocean to cool off.

He had just climbed into the Zodiac and was about to cast off when an air horn blasted and a familiar voice hailed him. "Ahoy, sailor!"

A sleek white speedboat entered the inlet where the Zodiac was anchored and glided alongside. The brunette who'd interrupted him and Nicole earlier stepped from the speedboat into the Zodiac. "We didn't have a chance to be formally introduced before," she said, offering her hand. "I'm Sandra Newman."

"Ian Marshall." He took her hand, but instead of shaking it, she held it for a long moment, and stroked her other hand down his bare arm.

"I'm pleased to meet you, Ian. You look even better up close than you did in the water."

He took a step back, out of her grasp. "It was nice meeting you, Ms. Newman. Now I have some things I have to do."

"But this is a deserted island. What could you possibly be rushing off to? Unless you're in such a hurry to see your girlfriend. When I left her, she was fawning over the handsome professor."

Ian had a difficult time picturing Nicole *fawning* over anyone, much less Adam. "Nicole and Adam are friends. They came to the island together."

"Friends, is it?" She lifted one eyebrow. "Is that what she told you?"

"Did you come all the way over here to play silly word games?" He moved past her and prepared to untie the Zodiac. Maybe if he started moving she'd get the idea and leave.

"You're right, that wasn't very nice of me." She sounded genuinely contrite. When he looked back, her expression was sober. "Maybe I'm jealous," she said. "I mean, one woman on an island alone with two gorgeous men? That's my idea of paradise."

He wanted to ask her what had brought her to the island, but he didn't want to get into any discussion about the treasure. No doubt she'd already talked to Adam and Nicole and Ian could get the story from them. He tried once more to get rid of her. "I really have to be going," he said, and started the Zodiac's outboard motor.

"Don't let me keep you." To his relief, she hopped out of the dinghy and splashed to shore. "I'll just take a little look around your camp while you're gone."

Without a backward glance, she started up the beach. Ian cut the engine and stared after her. "Stop. You can't just rummage through my private things."

She turned toward him and lowered her sunglasses to look at him. "But I'm a reporter. It's what I do."

Again she started up the beach. Ian quickly tied up the

Zodiac and hurried after her. "You've got a lot of nerve," he said, catching up with her.

"People have told me that before. It's a good thing, in my business."

"And what is your business on this island?"

"I told you before—I'm interested in the treasure Professor Carroway has found." She glanced at Ian. "Do you know anything about that?"

He looked away. "I don't know what you're talking about. You must have the wrong island."

She stopped so suddenly he almost collided with her. "I'm not an idiot, so don't try to treat me like one," she snapped. "I've already gone over this with the professor and your girlfriend, but I'll repeat it for you. I have a copy of the letter Adam sent to his friend at UM. I have a picture of the gold coin he found. I *know* there's a treasure here. And I'm going to make a documentary about it, whether you all cooperate or not."

It was quite a performance, all flashing eyes, heaving breasts and righteous indignation. Ian might have even been swayed, if he hadn't had the feeling it was all rehearsed, acted out for the benefit of invisible viewers. Sure enough, when he glanced back, a man was following them with a camera. "You're not going to have much of a documentary if all you get is footage of us arguing and scenic shots of coconut palms and ocean."

"I know that. Which is why I intend to film the shipwreck itself."

Ian shook his head. "Adam will never tell you where it's located. And you're not likely to find it on your own. After all, it was hidden for over three hundred years."

"I've made my career out of talking people into things they initially thought they didn't want to do." She leaned in closer, her tone seductive. "I can be very persuasive."

Maybe so. But Nicole had already persuaded him he wouldn't

be satisfied with any woman who wasn't her. Unlike Sandra, for whom he had the feeling seductress was merely another role in her arsenal of personas designed to get her what she wanted, Nicole had seduced him because he was what she wanted. Not the information he could give her or anything he could show her, but simply because he was who he was. She'd wanted his body.

That she might have gotten more—that she'd captured his mind and his emotions as well—was a complication he had shied away from examining too closely. They had only a few more weeks on the island together and he didn't want to spoil them by anticipating the pain that was headed his way when they finally parted.

Ian and Sandra reached his camp, the videographer trailing behind. "Isn't this adorable," Sandra exclaimed, taking in the fire ring, hut and hammock. "It looks like a set for *Gilligan's Island*." She walked to the edge of the shelter and turned, instinctively posing for a perfect shot. "Did you build all this?"

He nodded, and took up a position to one side, he hoped out of camera range as long as it was focused on Sandra.

She entered the hut and began looking through the books stacked on the table. "Botany, biology, zoology." She shook her head. "Is this why you came to a deserted island—to catch up on your reading?"

He said nothing and she moved closer to him. "You don't have to answer. I have research assistants in Jamaica. I'll radio them tonight and by tomorrow I'll know all about you." She laughed. "Why are you frowning? Does it bother you to know I'll be checking up on you? Don't you know we live in an era where there's no such thing as real privacy? The average person can find out anything she wants to know about you online." She patted his shoulder. "It makes it much more difficult to keep secrets."

With effort, he relaxed his expression, though he could do nothing about the tightening in his gut. His real life as an academic wasn't a horrible secret he wanted to conceal from the world, but it was one he had kept from Nicole. Not out of malice, but out of a perhaps misguided attempt to impress her. She seemed impressed all right—she saw him as a daring explorer who'd traveled the world. The truth about him would only suffer in comparison to that fantasy.

"Too bad the Internet won't help you find the treasure," he said.

Sandra's smile faltered. "I'll find the treasure," she said. "There are three people on this island who know where it is. One of you will let something slip, or I'll convince one of you to tell me all about it." She leaned closer once more. "It's a game I rather enjoy. If you play along, you could enjoy it, too."

Ian shook his head. "I think it's time for you to go."

She hesitated, then turned away. "I'll go, but I'll be back. We'll talk more later."

Ian watched her as she walked back to the beach, every sway of her shapely hips captured on camera. If she blew his cover, would that destroy whatever feelings Nicole had developed for him? If she knew he was an academic instead of an adventurer, would she reject him as Danielle had done? Had he lured her to fall for a false image, leaving no room for her to love him as he really was?

13

EVEN AFTER ALL THIS TIME on the island, the suddenness with which nightfall arrived still startled Nicole. One moment the sky would be bathed in the orange and red of a brilliant sunset, the next the sky would be the color of ink. No softening of light into dusk allowed for a gradual adjustment to the change; it was as if a curtain had suddenly been drawn, or a light switched out.

Normally, there would be no other lights visible from the yacht once darkness fell. Standing on the deck as she so often did in the evening, gazing out at the ocean, it was easy for Nicole to imagine she was alone on the island.

Tonight, however, the lights of Sandra's yacht glowed bright from its anchorage a few hundred yards out in the bay. Adam was belowdecks, stretched on his bunk and pretending to read, but really grumbling about his injury, the interruption of their salvage operation, his bad luck and who knew what else. Nicole had tired of listening to him and brought a drink up on deck.

She stared at those lights, trying to figure out why the arrival of this unexpected visitor annoyed her so much. She usually got along well with other people. She had welcomed Michelle and Bryan's visit and enjoyed their company. What was it about Sandra that felt so…threatening?

She sipped her drink and turned her back to the yacht. Did Sandra annoy her because the reporter was so glamorous and overtly sexy? Was it because some instinct told her the reporter was up to no good?

Or was it because Sandra Newman was everything Nicole had been pretending to be? She was a confident, assertive, take-charge kind of woman. A woman who knew what she wanted and went after it, whether it was a man or a job or the best table at a restaurant.

Nicole admired all those things. Since coming to the island, she'd been inspired to pretend she was that kind of woman. But deep inside she knew she was only playing a part. Sandra was the real thing.

Sandra *was* Passionata, or as close as anyone was likely to get in the twenty-first century. When Nicole was really honest with herself, she could admit that most of her ill feelings toward Sandra came down to jealousy.

And maybe a little worry. After all, Nicole-as-Passionata had seduced Ian. Now that the real thing had landed, would he still be interested in her imitation?

She walked to the other side of the yacht and searched the beach. Where was Ian? Maybe he wasn't coming. Maybe he'd been too tired or had decided to wait until morning.

Maybe he was with Sandra. Her hand tightened on the glass. Maybe that surgically enhanced bombshell was even now flirting with him, flattering him the way she had Adam. "Your picture doesn't do you justice." Please! Women didn't fall for those lines, why should men?

She heard a noise—the low growl of a motor—and turned out to sea. A light shone near the shore, growing larger and brighter as she waited. Soon she could make out the silhouette of the Zodiac, Ian in the stern, a marine flashlight in his hand.

He maneuvered the Zodiac alongside the yacht and tied up.

Nicole set her drink on the railing and met him at the top of the ladder. "Sorry I'm so late," he said. "I was delayed getting away from camp."

"It doesn't matter. Adam didn't want to wait and insisted on swimming out to the boat. Then I had to clean his wound all over again. But it doesn't look like it's getting infected."

Ian climbed on deck and glanced toward the cabin. "Is he asleep?"

"I don't know. I tried to get him to take some more pain medicine, but he said the pills muddled his thinking and he wanted to stay sharp."

"At least we have a few minutes alone." He pulled her close and kissed her—a passionate kiss that left her breathless and feeling triumphant. So much for thinking Sandra had distracted him.

"That was nice," she said when they finally parted.

He smiled and traced one finger along her jaw. "If we had the boat to ourselves I'd do more than kiss you."

"There's something to be said for anticipation." She pulled him close and they kissed again, the leisurely embrace of familiar lovers, an appetizer for greater indulgences later.

When they drew apart once more, Ian leaned against the rail, with Nicole still in his arms. "What delayed you?" she asked. "Did you have any trouble with the demiculveren?"

He shook his head. "But it took longer than I thought it would to hide it. It takes a lot of palm branches to conceal a bright-yellow life raft. I ended up painting the thing with mud to dull the color."

"Good idea. So you just now finished that?"

"No. I tried to leave earlier but our visitor waylaid me."

She frowned. "Sandra." She reached for her drink. "You know she's a big news celebrity in the United States."

"I didn't know that. She said she wants to film a story about the treasure. She said she had a copy of a letter Adam wrote."

Nicole drained her glass. "Yes. Someone at the university told her about it."

"What did Adam say about that?"

"I told her to piss off." Adam appeared at the top of the steps leading into the cabin. He clung to the railing with one hand and carried a bottle of rum in the other. "We'd better decide what we're going to do about this situation," he said, and limped to a trio of deck chairs arranged in front of a low table.

Ian and Nicole joined him, and Adam solemnly poured three drinks. "Is the demiculveren hidden well enough she won't find it?" he asked.

Ian nodded. "It's pretty far back in a swampy area, covered in mud and palm branches," he said. "Even from only a few feet away, I had trouble spotting it."

"Good. That's one less thing to worry about." He sipped his drink. "Now—how are we going to get rid of this nosy reporter?"

"Have you considered giving her what she wants?" Ian asked. "Why not show her the shipwreck? Let her film it and go on her way."

Adam shook his head. "Out of the question. Until I've established my claim to the wreck and secured funding for a salvage expedition, someone else could come in and steal everything. It's happened before."

"Until she leaves, we can't safely salvage anything else," Ian said. "She and that camera man will be following our every move."

Adam sat back and propped his injured leg on the table. "Then we wait her out," he said. "We go snorkeling. We hunt shells on the beach. Pretend we're ordinary tourists. A few days of that and she'll be bored out of her head and leave."

Nicole shook her head. "I don't think she'll leave."

"I agree," Ian said. "She doesn't strike me as the type of woman who'll give up easily."

"Maybe we could offer something as a decoy," Nicole said.

"What?" Adam looked around them. "Do you have a bunch of jewels or fake gold and silver coins we can pass off as the real thing? Besides, anything that would fool her would fool the real treasure hunters and thrill seekers, and the results would be the same—a bunch of interlopers swarming around the island."

"Then what are we going to do?" Nicole asked.

"Let's try waiting her out," Adam said. "If that doesn't work, we'll come up with a plan B."

"It better be a good one," Nicole said. "She's no dummy." And Sandra didn't strike her as the type of woman who was used to taking no for an answer.

SUCCESS BOUGHT MANY THINGS, not the least of which was rental of a luxury yacht, an army of people to cook, clean and do one's bidding, and a crack research assistant only a phone call—or in this case, a shortwave radio call—away. Sandra switched off the radio and sat back and sipped from the glass of champagne the steward, Rodrigo, had just delivered.

"What did you find out?" The cameraman, Jonas, stuck his head in the den that doubled as her office aboard the yacht.

She picked up the legal pad on which she'd made notes during her conversation with the researcher. "Professor Adam Carroway doesn't have a steady girlfriend that anyone knows about, but he isn't gay. He and Nicole Howard once shared a house but everyone is pretty sure they're nothing more than friends."

"What about the English dude?" Jonas leaned against the doorway.

Sandra smiled. "Ian Marshall. Assistant Professor Ian Marshall. Currently completing his doctoral studies in ecology and evolutionary biology at Oxford."

"So are Marshall and Carroway friends or colleagues or something?"

She shook her head. "I haven't figured out the connection."

"Unless it's the girl."

Sandra sipped more champagne and considered this. Nicole hadn't really struck her as the type who'd have two good-looking men in her thrall, but maybe there was something about her that really turned on these academic types.

"Nicole is a nurse," she said. "She recently was fired from a job at a surgical clinic. No one will say why, although one co-worker hinted at 'personal differences' with clinic management. No boyfriend waiting back home. Nothing remarkable about her at all."

"Except that she and Marshall are a hot item. At least, judging by how they were getting it on when we sailed up."

Sandra glanced at her notes again. "There is one interesting thing about Ian that I might be able to use. His trip here is apparently being funded by FREE—the Fund for the Rescue of the Earth's Environment."

"Is that one of those groups like Greenpeace?"

"Something like that. Apparently the British government is considering turning Passionata's Island into a military base and FREE is trying to stop them."

"Where does Marshall come in?"

"I'm not sure. His specialty is Caribbean ecology, so maybe they're hoping he'll come up with an endangered species or rare exotic plant that needs protecting."

"How does that help you?"

"I'm not sure. I'll have to think about it some more." She rubbed her bare arms, suddenly chilled, and reached for the gauzy cover-up she'd draped over the back of her chair.

"So what are you going to do?" Jonas asked. "We're wasting time and film following these three around."

"It's my time and film to waste." She gave him a hard look, reminding him exactly who was boss. "You follow them until I tell you not to. Meanwhile, I'm going to persuade either Ian or Adam to tell me where to find the treasure."

Jonas smirked. "You mean seduce."

"You use your terminology, I'll use mine." She finished off the champagne, the bubbles tickling her throat. "It all boils down to using one's talents to achieve a goal."

"And you're determined to get this story. But what if it turns out there's not much there?" Jonas folded his arms across his chest. "So far all we have is one coin."

"A gold coin. And if there's one, there's more. You saw the copy of that letter. It mentions coins, jewels, silver and other artifacts. Translation—riches. The kind of riches people fantasize about. The kind of riches they want to see on television. The special we did on the art collections of the rich and famous was the highest rated program in its time slot. This will be even bigger. It's a story with everything—pirates, deserted island, sexy men and women and treasure."

Jonas straightened. "If anyone can make them talk, you can. I just hope the end results are worth it."

"They will be." She smiled. "I have an instinct about these things."

She was more excited about this story than any she'd done in a long time. Not only did the prospect of capturing images of coins and chests spilling jewels intrigue her, but also she looked forward to practicing her powers of persuasion on not one, but two handsome men.

NICOLE EXPECTED SANDRA TO descend upon them once more the next morning, but as the sun rose toward its zenith there was still no sign of activity on the journalist's ship. Adam, made grumpier than usual by the pain in his leg and the frustration of not being able to continue salvaging items from the wreck of the *Eve,* napped fitfully in the shade of an awning over the deck.

"I'm going to collect coconuts," she finally told him, buckling on a machete.

"What are you going to do with them?" Adam asked, not bothering to open his eyes.

"I thought I might make some macaroons." Cookies seemed a good antidote to the restlessness Sandra's arrival had engendered.

Plus, the best coconut trees were on Ian's side of the island. They hadn't spent much time alone lately and she looked forward to renewing the physical side of their relationship. Sex was even better than cookies when it came to putting her in a good mood.

Unfortunately, Ian's camp was deserted. She searched along the beach but found no sign of him. He was probably out diving or taking photographs for the book he was writing or gathering food or any of the other half-dozen activities that no doubt occupied him when she wasn't around.

He could be visiting Sandra. She pushed the thought away, then drew her machete and slashed at a young palm tree, cleaving it in half.

After giving up on finding Ian, she collected half a dozen coconuts in the burlap sack she'd brought along and returned to the yacht. But as she climbed the ladder, she heard voices from the cabin—Adam and a woman, who could only be Sandra.

"Fine, if you don't want to talk about the treasure, let's talk about something else," Sandra said.

"What do you want to talk about?" Adam sounded wary, but he wasn't ordering her off the ship, so Sandra must have piqued his interest in some way.

"Tell me more about you. For instance, what's your relationship with your shipmate, Nicole?"

"Nicole and I are old friends."

"So there's nothing…intimate…between you?"

"No!" Adam sounded horrified at the idea. Nicole didn't know whether to laugh or be upset. She'd been just as horrified at the idea when Ian had suggested it shortly after they met. She and Adam had treated each other as brother and sister for so long that the idea of them as lovers was too close to incest.

Sandra laughed, a low throaty chuckle. "I only wanted to be sure. And I know that she and Ian are involved."

"How do you know that?" Adam asked.

She laughed again. "She didn't tell you? When my yacht entered the bay yesterday the two of them were fooling around in the water—stark naked."

Nicole winced. She wasn't ashamed that she and Ian were lovers, and Adam was smart enough to have figured that out anyway. But it was still embarrassing to have someone else relating details of her affair to him. Further proof she'd only been play acting the role of brazen seductress. She doubted Passionata, or Sandra for that matter, would ever be embarrassed at being caught in a tryst.

Speaking of embarrassed, she'd better not get caught eavesdropping. She started forward, intending to make some noise to let Adam and Sandra know she'd arrived, but Adam's next words stopped her. "I'm glad she's found a way to make this trip less boring."

"Is that what it's been for you, boring?" Sandra asked. "I would have thought finding the wreck of the *Eve* would be exciting—an important historical discovery."

"It is an important discovery," Adam said. "Too important to risk losing to every treasure hunter and adventurer who might see your program and rush to the island to poach on my claim."

"We could always work out an agreement not to air the film before you'd secured your claim."

"Why should I trust you?"

"Because I'm an honest woman."

Adam made a noise halfway between a bark and a laugh. But Sandra didn't take offense. "Think about what you know about me," she said. "I'm a woman who sets a goal and goes after it. I'm very forthright about my purposes. You may not agree with my methods, but you'll always know where you stand with me."

"And where do I stand with you?"

There was a long silence, and Nicole wondered again if she should interrupt. But curiosity won out over all the warnings she'd ever heard about eavesdropping. She set the bag of coconuts carefully on deck and tiptoed to the door, where she could hear the conversation more clearly.

"I find you very attractive," Sandra said. "You're both intellectual and rugged—qualities that in my experience make for an excellent lover."

"And you've had a lot of experience, I imagine."

"If you're trying to insult me, it isn't working," she said. "Yes, I've had experience. You have, too, I imagine."

"Hmmmph."

"I'll take that as a yes. Which leads me to wonder if the boredom you alluded to earlier in our conversation isn't really sexual frustration. I know if I spent the summer in a tropical paradise, forced by circumstance to be celibate, I wouldn't be a very happy camper."

"Are you offering to relieve my so-called frustration?"

"I'm sure we could have a very good time together."

The silence stretched again, longer and somehow conveying more than a lack of conversation. Nicole leaned around the edge of the door, peering into the cabin. She could make out Adam's hand resting on Sandra's hip, her arm reaching up around him.

Nicole straightened, red-faced. She had definitely heard—and seen—enough. Apparently, Adam was going to take Sandra up on her offer of "relief." Time to abandon ship.

She hurried across the deck, intending to climb down as quickly as possible. But she'd forgotten about the coconuts. She tripped over the bag and fell, sprawling, coconuts rolling around her.

"What the hell?" Adam exclaimed. A moment later he appeared in the doorway of the cabin looking distinctly disheveled.

Sandra peered around him. "What is it?"

Nicole sat up and waved weakly. "Hi. I didn't mean to interrupt."

"You weren't interrupting anything," Adam said. "Sandra was just leaving."

"I was?"

Adam moved out of the doorway. "Nice try," he said. "But you won't seduce the location of the treasure out of me, either."

Sandra glared at him. "For a man with a fancy degree, you aren't very smart."

"For a woman who's so honest, you're awfully good at lying."

Even furious, Sandra managed to look dignified as she stalked across the deck and climbed down the ladder. A few moments later Nicole heard the speedboat's motor roar, and the sleek craft raced out of the lagoon.

Nicole busied herself collecting the scattered coconuts. "What was that all about?"

Adam wiped a hand down his face. "I'm not sure." He shook his head. "I'm not sure." He retreated to the cabin once more, a man in a daze.

Nicole watched him leave, both concerned and amused. Adam didn't often lose his cool, especially when it came to women. Unlike some of his colleagues, who would sleep with anything in a skirt, Adam was very selective about his partners. As long as Nicole had known him, he'd kept his love life separate from his professional life. She could count on the fingers of one hand the women with whom he'd had more than one or two dates: the waitress from the café where he ate dinner regularly with whom he'd had an on-again, off-again romance for two years; a single mother he met at the dealership where he bought his last car, whom he'd dated for most of one year; a physician's assistant he'd met at a bar.

All the women had been quiet and unassuming, his intellectual inferiors. Nicole wasn't sure why none of the relationships had lasted, but maybe it was because none of the women really challenged Adam. He was a man who tested himself in his work and hobbies, but he'd always taken the path of least resistance when it came to women.

Maybe what Adam needed was a woman who would put up more resistance and keep him on his toes. A woman, as it happened, exactly like Sandra.

14

IAN FOUND SANDRA WAITING for him at his camp when he returned from snorkeling near the reef that afternoon. He'd spent the last several hours photographing a rare species of coral and intended to devote the rest of the day to writing up his notes. "I thought I told you to stay out of my camp," he said as he walked past the reporter, who'd made herself at home in a camp chair she'd apparently brought with her.

"I restrained my nosy impulses," she said. She stood and followed him into the shelter. "What have you been up to?"

"Don't you know already?" He hung his snorkeling gear to dry. "I thought you had spies following us all around."

She shrugged. "You spent the morning at the reef, taking photographs. Of fish, not treasure."

"Some people might argue the sea life and the reef are the island's real treasures," he said, pouring a cup of water.

"Your friends at FREE would say that, wouldn't they?"

He stared, trying to compose himself.

"Don't you think that glass is full enough?" she asked.

Water had overflowed the cup and was running across the table. He capped the water bottle and set it aside. "You've been busy," he said. "Yes, I have friends with FREE. What of it?"

"Not just friends—sponsors. They paid for this tropical vacation you're enjoying."

He took a long drink of water. Obviously, Sandra saw this as information she could use to her benefit, though he didn't see how. "What's your point?"

"I know about the British government's plans for Passionata's Island. I know FREE is working very hard to try to stop those plans going through. But it can be difficult to get the public excited about an uninhabited island hundreds of miles away from them. Fish and coral and odd little plants may interest scientists like you, but the average voter cares more about the price of gas and whether or not their soccer team is winning."

"Maybe you underestimate the average voter." Though he doubted Sandra underestimated much of anything.

"People don't read newspapers. There are so many people protesting different things these days the average person doesn't even pay attention anymore. But they do watch TV. They *especially* watch the kind of TV I produce."

"And what kind of TV is that?" he asked.

"Interesting TV. I offer them mystery. Beauty. Sex and violence."

"Pirate's treasure."

She smiled. "Exactly. I want to film the treasure Adam's found. You want to save this island. I think the two of us can help each other."

He shook his head. "I won't tell you where the treasure is located."

"No one has to know you told," she said. "You could, say, decide to go fishing one day. You'd just happen to fish over the site of the wreck. My spies would see you and I'd take it from there."

"And what do I get in return?" Not that he was considering that kind of betrayal of his friends, but he was curious what she thought she had to offer him.

"In return, I make a documentary about the island."

"A documentary with sex and violence."

Her smile was sly. "Picture this—we could recreate Passionata's reign with a bunch of scantily clad female pirates, then cut to modern times with women in bikinis on a sun-washed beach. We could put you in a Speedo and have you tell the audience all about the marine life, maybe show some footage of the reef. Viewers would love it, and the government would look like a bunch of idiots for wanting to turn the place into an air base."

He had no doubt she could make such a documentary. And that it would get people's attention. Michael Penrod and FREE would be ecstatic at the thought of that kind of publicity. For a moment Ian was tempted. But he shook his head. "No thanks."

Her expression turned cool. "You're making a big mistake."

He shrugged. "Maybe I am, but I'm not interested in selling out my friends for the sake of publicity."

"You mean selling out Nicole. Is that little nurse really so important to you?"

Sandra's dismissive tone angered him. "I think you'd better leave now," he said. "And don't come back."

She hesitated, then left. She took her time making her way to her boat, never looking back, though he was sure the exaggerated sway of her hips was for his benefit.

When she was gone, Ian sank into the chair she'd conveniently forgotten to take with her. She'd probably left it on purpose to give her an excuse to return. Just in case, he'd make certain his camera and important papers were locked away from her prying eyes whenever he left camp.

He'd have to compare notes with Adam and Nicole and see what tactics she'd used to try to persuade them to tell her about the shipwreck. She was definitely a creative thinker. The documentary was an angle he wouldn't have thought of himself. Though it was unsettling to know how much she'd learned about him in such a short time. He'd made no secret of his association with FREE, but he wouldn't have thought it was something that was well-known, either.

Maybe it wasn't that the information was so readily available, but that Sandra found a way to get the answers she was looking for. She had that kind of powerful personality.

Shaking his head, he reached for his notebook, intending to write up his findings from that morning's outing. But instead, his hand touched his copy of *Confessions of a Pirate Queen*. He fanned the pages, and they fell open to the passage he'd been reading two days before.

"I've never met a woman like you," William D. told me. We were lying in my bed one afternoon after making love. He had brought me to climax three times before I allowed his own release. It was an exhilarating experience for both of us.

"A woman as beautiful?" I teased him. "One who satisfied you so deeply?"

"One who wielded such power," he said. "It seems against a woman's nature to want to command a man."

It said much about the strength of his spirit that he was not afraid to say these things to me. "Every woman would wield such power if she realized what was to be gained by it," I told him.

"But why would you wish to do so?" he asked. "Why, when you might find a man who would give you everything you need and take care of you?"

"A caged bird may be well cared for, but is still confined to a cage." I shook my head. "I know what it is like to be powerless—at the mercy of what others decide for you, from what you shall eat to what you shall wear and where you shall go. I will never allow myself to be in that position again. Not for anything."

He looked at me curiously. Almost…pityingly. "Not for love?"

"Especially not for love. A love that desires to make a person a prisoner is no love at all."

Ian closed the book and laid it on the table once more. The conventions of her time had shaped Passionata's views on power and women's roles. She believed a woman's sexuality was her greatest power of all, but Ian thought William D. recognized an even greater power at any human's disposal. For love, people would risk everything, push themselves to the limit or humble themselves to the depths. People spoke of love making them "crazy" or "sick."

And love could change people, change the way they looked at the world and at themselves. Sex was part of love, but only one part. In the end it didn't matter so much who wielded the sexual power, but whether or not two people achieved a balance of power through love.

Nicole had told him she'd come to the island in the aftermath of an affair that had ended badly. She'd been intrigued by Passionata's theories, and Ian had been her willing partner in exploring these theories. But he was no William D. He wasn't ready to believe in a relationship built on one person dominating another—in or out of bed.

Nicole had come to mean more to him than a casual bed partner. Did she feel the same way? In the time they had left on the island, could they discover that greater power Passionata's consort had alluded to? Did Ian dare even risk suggesting they explore not only the power of sex, but the power of love?

NICOLE WAS WALKING along the beach when Sandra's speedboat raced by. The striking brunette was by herself in the craft, standing at the wheel, her figure shown to advantage in a bright-orange string bikini, her long hair flying behind her. The only thing missing from the picture was two or three muscle-bound sailors to worship at her feet.

Then again, maybe she was alone because, having been spurned by Adam, she'd decided to try her hand at seducing the island's other male inhabitant.

Annoyed at herself for obsessing over the idea, Nicole bent and scooped a handful of gravel from the beach and began lobbing the pebbles, one by one, into the lagoon. She told herself she had no real right to be jealous of Ian. They'd made no promises of fidelity to each other, though, since she was the only woman on the island until Sandra's arrival, fidelity had been assumed.

She tossed the last of the pebbles into the water and plopped onto the sand, knees hugged to her chest. "Why not admit you've fallen for the guy?" she mumbled to herself.

Passionata might write of never allowing love to enslave her, but despite her best efforts, Nicole had to admit she would never be a Passionata. She wanted the husband and family the pirate queen had forsaken. A real connection with a partner that demanded more equality. It was the thing that had been missing from her relationship with Kenneth, but swinging the pendulum the other way—so that she was always the one in power—wasn't any better.

Passionata might see love as a kind of slavery, but to Nicole it represented salvation.

Where did that leave her and Ian? She still suspected he was hiding something from her. The idea made her stomach hurt. He'd offered no further details about his work or background and, after her experience with Kenneth, wasn't her concern justified?

But was it Ian she doubted or herself—her own ability to have an equal relationship with a man?

"Are you one of those beautiful sirens I've read about?" a voice behind her asked. "The ones who lure men to perdition?"

She turned and found Ian walking toward her. He was smiling, relaxed as he dropped onto the sand beside her. There was nothing remarkable about his appearance or expression, and yet her heart fluttered wildly as she looked at him, as if she'd just stepped off the end of a pier and was waiting to hit the icy water.

He caught her in his arms and kissed her, a warm, intimate embrace as if only a few minutes, instead of days, had passed since they were last alone together. "I've missed you," he said, smoothing his hand down her arm.

"I've missed you, too."

He glanced toward Sandra's floating white castle. "Where were we before we were so rudely interrupted?"

"Mmmmm. Somewhere about here." She kissed him again. "But with less clothing between us."

He looked toward the yacht again. "Do you think she's watching?"

Nicole nodded. "She's probably filming us, too."

"I'm tempted to give her a free show, but that's not really my nature."

"What if that's what *I* wanted?"

"Is that really *your* nature?" He studied her a long moment, his eyes searching hers, as if her answer was really important to him.

"No." She looked down, suddenly embarrassed to reveal her former bravado had all been a sham.

He lifted her chin and looked into her eyes once more. "Let's go someplace more private," he said, his voice rough.

The simple words, and the urgency she saw in his eyes, made her feel hot and liquid. She nodded, then came out of her daze enough to say, "We'll have to go to your camp. Adam is on the boat."

"I had some place different in mind." The corners of his mouth tipped up in the beginnings of a smile.

"Oh? Where is that?"

"It's a hot day. Don't you think a cool shower would feel good?"

"A shower would feel good." She pulled him closer. "With you, I'll bet it would feel even better."

The three-sided shelter stood on a platform below and to one side of the cistern. A blue plastic tarp fitted with eyelets and strung on wire served as a curtain across the shower's opening, and a valve allowed the bather to control the flow of water through piping that ran from the cistern. Nicole and Ian mounted the steps to the platform and quickly shed their clothes and tossed them aside, then pulled the curtain around them. The sun filtered through palm branches, surrounding them with a greenish light. Here behind the curtain they were in a private world within the private world of the island.

They kissed, but there was a new urgency to the intimacy. Nicole hooked one leg around his hip and thrust her tongue deep into his mouth, wanting to be as close to him as possible. She needed him—right this moment if not sooner.

"Hey, slow down." He drew back a little and smiled at her. "We don't have to be in a rush. We have all the time we want."

But we don't, she thought. *Not really. We only have two weeks, and that will never be enough.*

He reached past her and turned the knob to open the valve. Warm water gushed from the tap, drowning out the call of the birds, caressing their bodies, flowing over and between and around them.

He slid his hands behind her head and lifted her hair, the wet strands flowing over his fingers. "You are so beautiful," he murmured. "If I were one of those long-ago sailors, I would have gladly drifted to my doom for a closer look at you."

"I wouldn't have let you die," she said. "I'd have been like Passionata. I'd have had to have you for my own."

"You have me now," he said. "For as long as you want me."

She stilled. Did he mean he was hers for as long as they were on this island? Or was he telling her he wanted to be with her even longer—after their summer here was done and it was time for them to return to the real world?

She had no time to contemplate this as he pulled her closer and kissed her once more. He traced his tongue along her mouth, then suckled lightly at her lower lip, exploring every sensitive nerve, before plunging his tongue into her mouth. She clutched at his hips to keep from sliding down, unsure if her legs could continue to support her. The onslaught of sensation left her weak and dizzy and wanting more.

He raised his head and smiled at her, then turned her so that her back was to him. "Let me wash you," he murmured, and reached for the sea sponge and the bottle of lilac-scented liquid soap she kept in the shower.

"Close your eyes," he whispered. "Don't think about anything but how good this feels."

She did as he asked, holding her breath in anticipation of his touch.

"Are your eyes closed?" he asked, his mouth very close to her ear. So close she felt his breath on her neck.

She nodded. "Yes."

"Good." His tongue traced the curve of her outer ear, and she let out her breath in a soft moan, immediately hot and wet for him.

The sponge, laden with suds, glided across her stomach and up her ribs to her breasts. Ian stroked the underside of each full mound, then dragged the sponge across her nipples, which tightened in response.

He slid the sponge lower, down her torso to her thighs and

around to her buttocks, which he stroked and smoothed. He traced the line of her spine, over one shoulder and back to her breasts. She leaned against him, eyes still tightly shut, every nerve burning with the need for him.

He dropped the sponge and slid soapy hands across her slick skin. He cupped her breasts, and traced their shape with his fingers, then devoted his attention to circling the nipples, plucking at them, drawing them out between his thumb and forefinger, then pressing them into her.

She moaned and leaned against him. "I don't know how much longer I can stand," she gasped.

In answer, he thrust his thigh between her legs, supporting her, but arousing her further still as he rubbed against her sex, which felt hot and heavy and very wet.

He slid his hands down to her stomach, then lower still to cradle her mons. She rocked against him, craving more contact. He obliged by dragging his thumb across her clit, and sinking his forefinger deep inside her.

"That feels amazing," she breathed.

"Mmmmm. It feels pretty great from this side, too." He slid his finger in and out, at the same time pulling her tighter against him, so that she could feel his erection pressed against the cleft of her buttocks.

She braced her legs farther apart, focused on the tension building within her at each slow stroke of his finger. He wrapped his other arm around her, and began kissing her neck and shoulder, feather kisses that sent fresh shivers of arousal down her back.

She was sure she would come at any moment, when he slid out of her. *"Nooo."*

He chuckled and kissed her cheek. "I'm not stopping altogether," he said. With his knee, he nudged her thighs apart. "Bend forward," he said. "Brace your hands against the wall."

She did as he asked, the water pouring across her back and rushing down her legs. Ian caressed and kneaded her buttocks, then she felt the head of his penis nudge her entrance. She widened her stance, encouraging him to enter her.

He did so, thrusting hard, sending a surge of intense pleasure through her. She moaned, and tightened her muscles around him.

He braced himself with one hand on her hip, the other coming up to fondle her breast. "Is this a good angle for you?" he asked, thrusting again.

"Yes." She gasped. With every forward thrust, her vision fogged, and she felt balanced on the edge of her climax. The combination of his hands and the water and the sharp angle of his thrusts intensified her arousal past anything she'd ever experienced before. She rested her cheek against the rough wooden wall and abandoned herself to the pure enjoyment of the moment.

Ian knew Nicole was close to coming. He felt the tension within her, the tightening of her muscles around his shaft, and noted the intensity of her expression. He moved his hand from her breast to her thigh, caressing her, reveling in the feel of her. In their brief time together, he had come to know her body well— its shape and how it responded to his touch. But he wanted to know so much more. He wanted the chance to discover how she looked and felt and reacted in every possible situation—to gain the knowledge that can only be obtained in a lifetime of loving.

He licked his fingers, then began to stroke her clit—slowly at first, encircling the hard bud, then withdrawing. He watched a rosy flush flood her features and heard the anxious rasp of her breath and his fingers moved faster, in rhythm with his thrusts.

She came with a keening cry, the force of her muscles tightening around him blurring his vision. He grasped her hips and sank into her deeper, harder, his own climax quaking through him before Nicole had even stopped trembling.

They clung together for minutes afterward, the only sounds those of the water rushing over them and their harsh breathing. Then Nicole straightened and he reluctantly slid from her, though he kept his arms around her, holding her close.

She turned to face him and kissed him, a deep, openmouthed expression of thanks and joy and so many emotions that couldn't be named.

"Every time with you is so incredible," he said when he could finally speak.

"Yes." She smoothed her hands down his chest, her expression solemn. "I'll probably forget a lot of things about this island when we leave here, but I won't forget this."

Her mention of their leaving was like a sudden drenching with cold water. In less than two weeks, friends would arrive to take him back to England. Nicole and Adam would return to the States, Adam to teach and to make plans to retrieve the rest of Passionata's treasure.

"What will you do when you return to the States?" he asked her.

She looked away. "I don't know. A nurse can always find a job."

How long before you find another lover? he wondered. But it was the kind of question that couldn't be asked. If he said anything at all, it would be to demand she come to England with him. That she continue as his lover and his friend.

But he couldn't utter those words, either. She had been very clear from the beginning about her desire for independence. And he couldn't forget her stated distaste for academics. He had enough pride left to want to avoid risking rejection.

If she wanted to stay with him, she would have to be the one to make that choice. As from the very beginning of their relationship, she would be the one to call the shots.

She turned away from him now and shut off the water. "I'd better go now," she said, and pushed aside the curtain.

She dried herself with her clothes, then put them on and walked away. Just as she had walked away that first night, when she'd left him in the hammock. Ian clenched his hands into fists and stared after her. She acted as if nothing had changed between them since that first night.

But that was a lie. So much had changed. He had arrived here nursing the wound of Danielle's rejection, unsure of himself and his capabilities as a man. Forced to rely on his own resources, he had discovered emotional and physical strengths he never knew he possessed. And he had discovered a capacity to connect with a woman in a way he'd never even imagined before. After his time here on the island with Nicole, he knew he would never be the same.

15

NICOLE HAD TO LEAVE Ian before she embarrassed herself by crying. Making love to him had been so beautiful. How was she going to give that up?

When he'd asked what she intended to do when she returned home, she'd hoped he would ask her to come back to England with him. But he hadn't. Whatever secrets he kept about his life there would remain secret to her.

She was still feeling miserable when she returned to the yacht. Adam greeted her at the rail. "Where have you been?"

She moved past him, toward the cabin. "I went for a walk."

"A walk over to Marshall's camp?"

She stopped. "What difference does it make to you?"

"Ordinarily none, but I don't want to see you hurt. After all, you're rebounding off one bad relationship."

Did he have to remind her? She turned. "Do you think I'm that bad a judge of men?"

"I didn't mean it that way." His expression softened. "I've known you a long time, so I know a little bit about you. When you fall for a guy, you fall hard. You put everything into a relationship. But guys don't always return the favor—and you get the short end of the deal. I don't want to see that happen again."

His concern was touching, but his words also dismayed her. "So you think Ian doesn't care about me?"

"I don't know the man well enough to say, one way or another." He leaned toward her. "But I'm getting the feeling you're starting to really care for him and I see a lot of problems with that."

"What kind of problems?"

"How about the fact that he lives in England and you live in the U.S.? Not exactly an easy commute for a date or a quick weekend together. Then there's the fact that you met on a tropical island with no one else around. A fantasy situation that might not carry over so well into the real world."

He wasn't saying anything she hadn't already thought about, still, it stung to hear. She turned away and busied herself adjusting the angle of a deck umbrella over one of the lounge chairs. "You don't have to worry about anything. Ian and I are out to have a good time. The fact that we know this isn't something we can continue once we leave the island is a plus." Or it had been in the beginning. Somehow in the past few weeks, that had changed.

She could feel Adam's gaze on her, his silence more weighted than his words. She turned to him again. "What?"

He shook his head. "Nothing. But listen, don't get too settled in that chair."

"Why not?"

"I want to go out in the Zodiac."

"Why? Where?"

"I'm sick of being cooped up here on this ship. And I want to frustrate Sandra and her spies a little."

If Nicole had had any doubt that the journalist had gotten under Adam's skin, it was erased when he said her name. His voice had a strained quality, and something like desperation flitted through his eyes. "What are you going to do?" she asked.

"Bring your snorkeling gear and some markers. We'll make her think we're at the wreck site."

Nicole laughed. It was a simple, yet devious exercise, one she was only too happy to take part in.

With Adam manning the rudder, they took the Zodiac out to deep water, well away from the actual wreck site. While he opened a notebook and made a show of taking GPS readings, Nicole donned her snorkeling gear and swam around, setting markers. They hadn't been in place five minutes before the white speedboat anchored a few hundred yards away. Nicole treaded water and watched as a man aimed a video camera in their direction, while Sandra sunned herself on the deck.

Nicole swam back to the boat. "Looks like we fooled her," she said as Adam helped her back into the boat. "Though probably not for long. I imagine as soon as we leave she'll have someone diving around our markers, to see what's there."

"It'll keep her occupied for a while, anyway." He stretched his leg out in front of him and stared glumly at the line of stitches snaking down his thigh.

Nicole leaned over him to check her handiwork. "It looks good. You'll have a nice scar you can make up stories about, but other than that, no ill effects."

His expression didn't lighten any. "We've only got two more weeks here to salvage what we can from the wreck," he said. "We've got to find a way to get rid of that woman and her spies so we can get to work."

"I don't know what we can do until she decides to leave." She smiled. "Too bad we can't arrange a convenient shark attack on one of her divers. That might scare her off."

Adam nodded, deep in silence. Suddenly he looked up, his face radiating fevered excitement. "That's it. We'll scare her off."

"What are you talking about? Do you have a few trained sharks around?"

"Not sharks. We'll tell her the island is haunted." He rubbed his hands together. "If she's done her research, she'll have heard of Passionata's curse. We'll build on that—tell her we've seen ghosts, found bones—whatever sounds creepiest."

Nicole crossed her arms beneath her breasts and studied her friend. "If this place is so creepy, how are you going to explain away the fact that the three of us have spent all this time here?"

"They've left us alone mostly because there are only three of us," he said. "But now Sandra has brought all these other people along and the ghosts are freaked out about it."

"And we know this how?" she asked. "Sandra isn't merely going to take your word for it. She's going to want to see proof of this supposed haunting."

"I've already thought of that." He gunned the motor and headed toward shore. "I've got a recording of whale songs and a tape recorder," he said, shouting over the engine noise. "If you set the player on a slow speed, the whales sound like they're moaning. It's very creepy. We can hide it in the tower and have it playing while I'm showing Sandra around."

Nicole shook her head. "I don't think it will work. If anything, the idea of a curse and haunting could make her even more anxious to film a story about the island and the treasure."

"It will work." Adam set his mouth in a stubborn line. "If it doesn't scare her, maybe it will frighten her crew enough to make them want to leave."

"But what if it doesn't work?"

He glared at her. "It will work. It has to."

She shook her head but made no further objections. Adam was as single-minded about this as he was about everything else. He'd wanted to find Passionata's treasure, so he'd found it. He wanted Sandra to leave, so he was going to find a way to get rid of her. "What do you want me to do?"

"We'll ask Ian to invite Sandra and her crew to dinner at his camp—the kind of get-together we had when Bryan and Michelle were here. While everyone is drinking and having a good time,

I'll plant the player in the tower and rig up a few other surprises. After supper, we'll tell our ghost stories and set the mood for the haunting."

"It sounds like a fun party, if nothing else," Nicole said. She didn't believe for a minute it would discourage Sandra, though.

IAN DIDN'T MISS THE irony of a man who never entertained in his London apartment throwing his second party of the summer on a "deserted" island. When Adam had presented his plan to try to frighten Sandra and her film crew off the island, Ian had been skeptical, but agreed to go along. He avoided having to visit Sandra on her boat by passing along the invitation to one of her cameramen who had followed him on a snorkeling expedition on the reef.

By the time Adam limped into camp with Nicole, Ian had set the stage for a haunted evening. He'd arranged torches around the perimeter of the area and laid a fire in the pit. On the table, out of the reach of land crabs and other pests, was a tub full of fish he'd caught and cleaned that afternoon, ready to grill for the guests.

"I brought a salad," Nicole said, handing over a mix of local greens, hearts of palm and a coconut dressing. "And coconut cake."

"I brought the sound effects." Adam held up the player. "Instead of setting it up in the tower, I thought I'd attach it to a tree nearby."

"He just wants to avoid being alone in the tower with Sandra," Nicole said.

Adam's cheeks reddened. "I thought she might get the wrong idea if I suddenly suggested a visit to the tower after dinner," he said.

"I understand completely," Ian said. "The woman is a barracuda."

"Speaking of barracudas, do you have any pictures of the

ones we spotted around the wreck?" Adam asked. "We need something that doesn't show the wreck itself, of course."

"I think I have some. Why?"

"I convinced him that a ghost wasn't going to be enough to scare Sandra off," Nicole said. "So we've decided to emphasize all the natural hazards of the area, too. If she's out of her element anywhere, it has to be out here in the middle of nowhere surrounded by sharks, barracudas, land crabs and whatever else we can come up with."

"Are there any poisonous snakes here?" Adam asked.

Ian shook his head. "I don't think so. I certainly haven't seen any."

Adam frowned. "What about big, hairy spiders?"

"*Oooh.*" Nicole hugged herself. "No spiders, please!"

Ian grinned. "I might be able to come up with some spiders for you. And don't forget wharf rats. They're really nasty and sometimes carry the plague."

"Now you're freaking *me* out," Nicole protested. She turned toward the table of food. "I see you've got some green bananas."

"I thought we'd roast them like plantains," Ian said, going along with the change of subject.

Nicole nodded. "I hope they get here soon. I'm starved."

He studied her back, wishing she'd turn toward him. She hadn't looked him in the eye even once since they'd parted company this morning. He felt the distance between them and wanted to ask her what he'd done or said that had led to this sudden coolness. But until they were alone again, he could only try to hide his frustration.

They heard the speedboat's motor approaching, and a few minutes later Sandra strode up the path from the beach. She wore a white wrap dress that showed off every curve, and beaded sandals that would have been at home on a Paris street. Behind her came half a dozen men, each carrying something: a chair, the video camera, a cooler, a beach umbrella and a crate of wine bottles. The last man in the train bore a gold candy box.

Ian suppressed a laugh. The woman certainly knew how to make an entrance.

"Is that Godiva?" Nicole asked, gaping at the last man.

"Of course." Sandra smiled. "I never go anywhere without plenty of chocolate and champagne." She indicated the crate. "And I'm always happy to share."

Nicole looked at the other woman with a new measure of respect.

Ian invited them all to sit. Sandra's helpers set up the umbrella and her chair, while two more opened and served the champagne. Nicole buried the bananas in the ashes to bake and Ian began broiling the fish, while Adam stationed himself beside the fire with a boat oar.

"What are you doing with that?" Sandra asked. Ian had wondered the same thing.

"The land crabs around here are vicious," Adam said. He brandished the oar. "They'll devour anything they think is food. I've seen them try to drag dinner right out of the fire."

"It's a wonder there are so many of them, if they're that dumb," Sandra said.

"They're primitive creatures," Adam agreed. "Eating machines. They've been known to eat men alive."

"No!" This definitely got Sandra's attention. Nicole was also gaping at him.

He nodded solemnly. "Sailors have always dreaded being washed ashore injured or too weak to fend for themselves. Such poor souls would be besieged by hoards of land crabs and eaten alive."

"That's disgusting." Sandra sipped her champagne. "I've been all over the beach here and I haven't been attacked."

"Just don't fall asleep on the beach," Ian said, getting into the spirit of the tale. "You might wake up minus a toe."

Nicole coughed, her hand over her mouth. "That—that's terrible!" she said. She cleared her throat. "You two need to stop it. You're going to frighten our guests."

Sandra dismissed the idea with a wave of her manicured fingers. "I've heard worse. After all, I work in television."

Ian wasn't sure what she meant by this but let it pass.

They managed to cook the fish with no threats from land crabs, though Adam stood at the ready with his oar the whole time. When Ian pronounced the fish done, Nicole served up plates of baked bananas, fish and salad. With cake and chocolate for dessert, and plenty of champagne, it was a feast fit for royalty.

Adam eased into a sitting position on the ground with his plate, groaning. "Are you all right?" Sandra asked.

He grimaced, but nodded. "I'm fine. Just this shark wound still bothers me."

She leaned over to get a better look at the line of stitches on his thigh. "You never did tell us what happened," she said. "Where were you attacked?"

"Not far from shore," he said. "There were two of them actually. One attacked while the other circled, waiting for his turn. If I hadn't shot them, I'd probably be dead now."

It was close enough to the truth that Ian didn't have to act when he expressed his concern. "I was there," he said. "It's amazing how fast the bastards are. And totally fearless."

"Be careful when you're swimming or snorkeling," Nicole added. She turned to the man next to her, one of the cameraman. "You especially need to be careful with any kind of electronic device underwater. Something about the electrical impulses is said to attract them."

The man paled. "Electronic devices?"

"Like video cameras," Adam said. "Tape recorders. Depth finders. That kind of thing." He stripped a fish bone of meat and tossed it toward the outskirts of their circle. As if on cue, a crab scuttled forward and snatched it up.

Sandra shuddered. "I don't think you ought to encourage them to hang around," she said.

Adam shrugged. "If they don't clean up, the rats will."

"Rats?" asked one of the other men.

"Wharf rats," Ian said. "Huge things, as big as squirrels. They gnawed through one of my trunks the first week I was here." This was absolutely true. He'd learned to put his food in metal containers after that.

"Of course neither the rats nor the crabs are as bad as the wolf spiders," Ian continued.

"Wolf spiders?" a third man asked.

Ian nodded solemnly. "*Lycosa lugubris*. Some of them grow as large as a man's hand." He spread his fingers wide to illustrate. "Their venom can cause paralysis. Plus, they have a nasty habit of leaping out at their victims from trees." This last was complete fiction, but he thought it was a nicely horrific touch.

Most of the company—including Nicole—looked suitably horrified. Sandra, however, only smiled. She tossed a fishbone to one side and watched a crab carry it away. "I know what you're trying to do," she said. "But I told you, I don't scare easily. Besides, if it was so awful here, the three of you wouldn't stay."

"We're only trying to warn you about what you'll have to deal with if *you* decide to stay," Adam said. "We've accepted the hazards and have managed to deal with them—so far."

Her crew members didn't look nearly as confident in their ability to cope.

Dinner done, they each had a slice of cake, then Sandra passed around the box of chocolates. Nicole selected two pieces and nibbled at the first. Eyes closed, she let out a moan that caused an immediate response in Ian's groin. Maybe it was true that some women enjoyed chocolate almost as much as sex.

Adam didn't seem to notice. He stood. "Excuse me a moment," he said, and hobbled toward the trees.

"Where's he going?" Sandra asked.

Ian coughed. "I imagine he's going to, um, use the facilities."

Sandra laughed, then called over her shoulder. "Watch out for the wolf spiders!"

He returned shortly and poured the last of the champagne into their glasses. Sandra settled more comfortably into her chair and fixed them all with a benevolent smile. "Tell me more about this treasure," she said.

"Your favorite topic," Adam said, emptying his glass.

Her smile broadened. "Of course. And I imagine yours, too. At least when I'm not around."

"We're not going to tell you anything, so why do you keep bringing it up?" Nicole asked.

"Because I know that in two weeks, Professor Carroway has to report back to the University of Michigan, and Ian has to return home, as well." She leaned forward. "I'm prepared to sit here the entire time and wait you out. You won't be able to do anything without me or one of my crew knowing it, so why don't you give up now and show me what you've got?"

"We can't do that," Adam said.

"Don't be ridiculous. Nothing's stopping you."

He shook his head. "We can't. It would be too dangerous."

"Dangerous?" Sandra frowned. "You're not making sense."

He traded knowing glances with Nicole. Ian nodded, playing along.

"It would be too dangerous for you," Adam said.

"Let me guess—the sharks? Or is it something else this time? A giant clam or a woman-eating octopus?"

Adam's expression remained grim. "I can't tell you about the treasure because of the curse."

"A curse!" Sandra's laughter was harsh in the silence that followed. "That's rich. A curse. Couldn't you have come up with something better than that?"

"It's no laughing matter," Adam said. "You've heard, of course, of Passionata's curse?"

"Some nonsense uttered on the gallows, wasn't it?"

Adam settled onto the sand once more. "Passionata, the pirate queen, reigned on this island for sixteen years," he said. "She was one of the most accomplished, and feared pirates of her day—or any since. All kinds of rumors circulated about the treasure she'd accumulated. After she was captured, the British overran the island and searched, but found little."

He leaned forward, and poked at the fire with a stick. Sparks flew upward, bright orange in the blackness. Adam continued, his voice low, mesmerizing. "Just before she was hanged, Passionata was asked if she had any last words. She said yes, and was allowed to step forward.

"Picture her—she's been described as not a beautiful, but a striking woman. Tall for the time, with a good figure and rich, red hair that was probably hennaed. She would have been modestly dressed in a plain-colored gown, but I've no doubt her regal bearing that had come from years of commanding others, including a good many men, had everyone in the crowd riveted on her."

He straightened, assuming a more professorial tone. "The actual words of her curse are unknown, but the gist of her message was that Passionata's Island belonged to her and her alone, and that none other should ever possess it or the treasure it contained. Anyone attempting to do so would be cursed and eventually destroyed."

No sound greeted these words except their breathing and the crackle of the fire. Sandra spoke first. "It's a good story. I should use it for my film. Whoever came up with it has a talent for fiction." She fixed Adam with a steely gaze.

Adam shook his head. "I'm not a superstitious man, but I've seen enough since we came here that I believe in the curse. And history bears me out. Every attempt to settle this island has been met with failure in the form of disease, famine or destruction by storms." He proceeded to enumerate the various settlement attempts with dates and the cause of destruction, as if he was lecturing to a class that would later be tested on the subject.

"And then there's all the trouble we've had since coming here," he said. "Sickness, equipment breaking or simply disappearing. And now a shark attack."

"You're exaggerating in another attempt to scare me off," Sandra said. "I don't believe any of it."

"You can't deny I was attacked by sharks."

She shrugged. "I don't believe it was because of a curse."

"That still doesn't explain the ghost," Nicole said quietly.

All attention focused on her. She shifted in her chair, as if uncomfortable with their attention. "A ghost?" Sandra's voice held laughter.

"At night, there are…voices." Nicole's gaze darted toward the jungle. "And mysterious sounds." She shuddered.

Right on cue, Adam's recording kicked in. Ian would have to congratulate him on the timing. The sounds started off low, like wind rushing over the neck of a bottle, then quickly rose in intensity. There was something primal and pain-filled about the cries. The hair rose on the back of Ian's neck and goose flesh stood out on his arms.

One of the crewmen stumbled to his feet. "We should go back to the ship."

The others murmured agreement and began gathering their belongings. "Calm down, all of you!" Sandra's voice crackled with impatience.

The men froze. "It's a trick," she said, and pointed to Adam. "He's probably planted a recording out there in the jungle."

"You're welcome to look." Adam faced her, arms folded across his chest, expression placid.

Sandra nodded to the man closest to her. "Go look for the player."

The man stared at her, then shook his head. "No way. You don't pay me enough to go out there with the crabs and rats and spiders and God knows what else."

"Fine. Then I'll go." She shoved herself out of her chair.

Adam grabbed her arm as she tried to move past him. "I'd really hate to see you hurt."

"You're a terrible liar." She pulled away from him and plunged into the jungle.

The others remained frozen and silent, listening to the sounds of thrashing and cursing as Sandra fought her way through the dense undergrowth. This went on for some time. Nicole glanced at Adam. "Maybe you ought to go get her," she said.

Adam opened his mouth, but before he could answer, the stillness was shattered by a blood-curdling scream.

16

IAN AND ADAM RACED toward the sounds of struggle. Ian arrived first, Adam at his heels. They found Sandra thrashing around clawing at her face. Her hair hung in her eyes and her arms were scratched. She was breathing hard and cursing the air blue. Adam took her by the shoulders and shook her. "It's okay," he said. "I'm here. What happened?"

"Sp-spiderweb!" she gasped, raking a hand through her hair.

Adam brushed her face and came up with a handful of sticky web. "You probably walked right into it."

"Good thing there wasn't a spider on it," Ian said.

Sandra glared at him. "How do you know there wasn't a spider?"

He shrugged. "You'd have felt the bite by now."

She looked sick. "Nothing bit me, but something ran across my foot."

"Probably a rat," Ian said. He knew he should be more sympathetic, but he was having difficulty holding back his laughter. The poised seductress of a moment before had been reduced to a flustered mess.

Adam led the way back to camp, keeping hold of Sandra's arm. She took advantage of the situation by leaning into him, but Adam made no protest. And why should he? Ian told himself

Sandra was a beautiful woman and, unlike Ian, Adam had spent a celibate summer.

At camp Sandra moved away from Adam and straightened, managing to regain her dignity despite her disheveled appearance. "Pack up," she ordered her crew. "We're leaving." She looked at Adam. "Not the island, just the camp. Don't think you've won. I meant what I said about waiting you out."

She stalked away, her crew trailing behind. One even remembered to take the chair Sandra had previously left at the camp. "I wonder how she'll feel about things in the morning," Ian said.

"Probably more determined than ever," Nicole said. She began gathering up drink glasses. "I have to admit, I admire her nerve. And there are brains behind those showy looks. She's not the bimbo I thought she was the first day I saw her on that yacht."

"You're just saying that because she brought you chocolate," Adam said. He began shoveling sand onto the fire to douse it. "We'll wait and see what happens next. Maybe she'll have nightmares about spiders all night and decide running after a mythical treasure isn't worth it."

"Spiders." Nicole shuddered. "Do they really leap out of trees?"

Ian laughed. "No. And I don't think they're poisonous either, except to their prey and the occasional person who has an allergic reaction."

"I'll be lucky if *I* don't have nightmares now," she said. "Focusing on the creepy crawlies was definitely scarier than curses and ghosts."

"Thanks for all your help," Adam said to Ian. "Dinner was great." He stretched his arms over his head and yawned. "I'm going back to the yacht."

"Let me finish cleaning up here and I'll come with you," Nicole said.

"You don't need to hurry." He patted her arm. "Just...be careful." Then he lumbered off down the path.

Adam helped Nicole with the dishes. "What was he telling you to be careful about?" he asked.

She shrugged, avoiding his gaze. "I guess he didn't want me encountering any spiders or rats."

Ian didn't think she was telling the truth. Adam had been warning her—maybe about Ian himself. He took her hand and pulled her over to the log seats by the now-cold fire. "The dishes can wait," he said. "Right now we need to talk."

She nodded. "Yes, we do. There's something I have to tell you."

"Me first." He put up his hand. He had to get this out before he changed his mind. "I'm afraid I might have given you the wrong impression about me."

She jerked her head up and looked at him directly for the first time all evening. "What do you mean?"

He took a deep breath. "You thought I was a world traveler. An adventurer. But I'm not. In fact, this is the first time I've been more than fifteen minutes from a coffee shop in my life."

She stared at him, apparently trying to digest this information. "But you are writing a book," she said finally.

"Not exactly." He laced his fingers together, staring at the entwined digits as if that would help him figure out how to make this any less damning. "I have been doing research here, and a lot of writing—that part was true. But I'm not writing a book. I'm working on my doctoral thesis on the ecology of the Caribbean." He risked looking at her. "I'm an associate professor at Oxford. And I'm here on the island on behalf of an environmental group, the Fund for the Rescue of the Earth's Environment, more commonly known as FREE. They're trying to stop development of the island and hoped my documentation of rare plant and animal life would help their cause."

She stared at him, clearly in shock. Ian felt sick. "I'm sorry I didn't tell you sooner," he said.

"Why didn't you?"

He shook his head. "One of the oldest reasons in the world, I guess. You're a beautiful woman and I wanted to impress you. That first day, you spoke so disparagingly about intellectuals and academics—I didn't want you to think those things about me before we even had a chance to know each other. So I let you think things that weren't exactly true."

"You lied."

He winced. "It really wasn't such a big lie. I mean, what I do back in England didn't seem that important here in this place."

"But you lied." She stood. "I thought I knew you, as well as I could know anyone. Now I found out I didn't know anything."

"You do know me. The man you've been with is the real me. Teaching is just a job." He reached for her, but she moved away.

"You let me think what I did because it made you look good. Maybe it was all part of the game we were playing, acting out our fantasies here on this island."

"That's right," he said, taking hope from her words. "It was part of the game. I never meant to deceive you."

"But you did deceive me." She looked at him again, her eyes bright with tears. "We're not playing a game anymore, Ian. I...I have feelings for you. But now I don't know if they're for you, or for some imaginary man you were pretending to be."

"They were me," he said, desperate to convince her. "The man who made love to you—the one you laughed with, the one who held you and kissed you—that was the real me."

She shook her head. "I don't know that. I don't know what to believe anymore." She turned and fled. He took a few steps after her, then stopped, his whole body feeling as if it were made of lead. Nothing he could say to Nicole now would convince her that he hadn't been hiding parts of his personality from her. Nothing would make her believe he was telling the truth when he said he loved her.

NICOLE SOMEHOW MANAGED to dry her tears by the time she got back to the yacht, but she knew as soon as she was secure in her own cabin the waterworks would start again. How could this be happening to her again? How could she have fallen for yet another man who wasn't what he'd first appeared to be?

She climbed the ladder to the yacht and started across the deck, only to be stopped by a voice from the darkness behind her. "You're back earlier than I thought you'd be."

She turned and saw Adam seated in one of the lounge chairs. "I didn't realize you were still up," she said, stalling, trying to compose herself.

"I thought maybe you'd spend the night with Ian," he said.

"I…" She swallowed a fresh knot of tears. "I don't think I'll be seeing Ian anymore. At least…not that way."

"What happened?"

Almost any other person, she would have shrugged off the question with a terse "Nothing," or "I don't want to talk about it." But Adam might be the only person she could ever talk to about this—the only one who knew both her and Ian. He was one of her dearest friends, one who could offer a man's point of view and a cool, unemotional perspective. She walked over and sat at the end of his lounge chair. "He finally told me what he's been doing on the island all this time."

"Oh? Is he trying to steal my treasure after all?"

"No. He's writing a doctoral dissertation on the ecology of the Caribbean and collecting information for an environmental group that's trying to stop the British government from developing the island."

"Is he? No wonder he knew so much about the local flora and fauna—and spiders."

She nodded.

Adam leaned toward her. "What's the problem? Has being around me soured you on academics forever?"

She couldn't help but smile at his teasing tone. "No. But Ian led me to believe he was this great adventurer and writer. He lied to me."

Adam sat back and said nothing for a long moment. "Not to mince words, but coming here for three months on his own would seem to make him an adventurer—not to mention the whole thing of taking on the British government as part of this environmental group. I've known a few protesters like that and it's not work for the faint of heart. And a dissertation is writing— more work than most books, I'd imagine."

Nicole stared at him. "I can't believe you're taking his side."

"I'm not taking anybody's side. I'm just trying to get the facts straight in my mind. What else did he do to upset you?"

"That's it. But isn't it enough?"

"Obviously. You're upset. Do you think he was just telling you what you wanted to hear to get you in bed? I hope you're not shocked to hear he wouldn't be the first man to try something like that."

She hugged her arms across her stomach, as if doing so might somehow contain her pain. "I don't think it was that." After all, *she'd* been the one to proposition *him*. And if she were being completely, painfully honest with herself, she had to admit she'd been playing a role in this relationship as well.

The fact that his deception had hurt her while she'd never considered her own dishonesty dismayed her. In spite of all her efforts to change, could it be she was still the passive, compliant woman at heart who wanted to be wooed and courted by some mythical perfect man?

Ian had admitted wanting to impress her. Was that so different from her own desire to show off her own strength and independence? The adventurer thing had been merely an added attraction. "I'm just getting over one man who lied to me," she said, stubbornly clinging to her hurt. "I don't want to get involved with another one like that."

"Do you think Ian has been cheating on you? With Sandra?"

She shook her head. "I don't think so." This morning she would have said she was certain Ian wasn't interested in Sandra, but now how could she be certain of anything?

"Her ego is probably crushed, having two men turn down her advances." He looked across the water, to the lights illuminating the larger yacht. "I wish I could find some way to make her leave me in peace."

Nicole seized on this chance to change the subject. "She's not going to give up," she said. "She hasn't gotten to where she is by giving up."

"I've done everything short of begging her to go," he said. "I'm almost willing to try that next."

"Or you could show her the treasure."

"I told you I can't do that. If she makes that documentary of hers, this place will be crawling with would-be treasure hunters and the modern-day equivalent of pirates out to usurp my claim on the wreck."

"I'm not so sure of that." An idea that had been forming in the back of her mind for a while suddenly crystalized. "Think for a minute about what you have to show her."

Adam frowned. "There's the demiculveren, the fragments of china I think may have been part of a special set commissioned by the British Royal Navy—that would be a real find—a silver flask and some other small items. Even one of them would have researchers and museums drooling, though the cannon is probably the most impressive."

"To researchers and museums maybe, but to a woman like Sandra, I'm thinking not so much."

Adam still looked confused. "What are you getting at?" he asked.

"Show Sandra everything you've found so far," she said. "I'm betting she won't find anything television-worthy."

He considered the idea for a moment. "It's a big risk."

"You still have the option of not revealing the shipwreck's location. But I'm betting once she sees your precious artifacts, she'll pack up and sail back home."

"All right. We'll give it a try. We'll talk to Ian in the morning about getting the demiculveren out of hiding."

Ian again. She felt a physical pain in her chest at the mention of his name. No matter her own guilt in this affair, his deception seemed far larger in her mind. The bottom line was she couldn't trust him, and without trust, there was no relationship. She didn't know how she was going to get through the coming days without breaking down in front of him, but she'd manage somehow.

Passionata wouldn't have wasted sentiment over a man. The pirate queen used men for her pleasure and kept her heart as independent and unfettered as the rest of her. Nicole saw the idea's appeal and had tried to put it into practice. But she'd discovered she was not the type to keep body and soul separate for long. She'd shared her body with Ian and given away her heart in the process. She was no Passionata, just a woman in love with the wrong man. Again.

IAN WAS SURPRISED BY Adam's request to bring the demiculveren out of hiding, but once he heard the plan, he agreed with Nicole that this might be the thing to put Sandra off doing her documentary. To an historian like Adam, the items they'd brought up from the wreck were priceless treasures, but to a woman like Sandra—and to her viewers—they'd look like refuse sifted from the town dump.

Under full view of Sandra and her men, Ian, Adam and Nicole uncovered the ship's gun and floated it around to Adam's yacht, where they spent the better part of the morning loading it on board with the help of a block and tackle, a winch and much straining and yelling.

They'd barely lashed it into place on deck when the white motorboat drew alongside. "What have you got up there?" Sandra called.

"Come up and see," Adam answered.

Sandra and a cameraman boarded the yacht. While the camera man focused on the demiculveren, Sandra turned to Adam. "Is this one of the cannons from the *Eve?*"

"It's a demiculveren." Adam stroked the corroded barrel of the brass gun. "They didn't call them cannons."

Sandra walked around the gun, eyeing it critically. "Couldn't you polish it up a bit? It looks awfully dirty."

"I'll leave the restoration to the experts," Adam said. "It's a time-consuming process and it has to be done carefully to preserve as much of the original gun as possible."

She shrugged and turned away from the gun. "I'm glad to see you've given up trying to stonewall me. What else have you salvaged from the wreck?"

"We have some small personal items from the ship that are of particular interest." Adam led her to a table where he'd laid out their stash of artifacts. The collection of broken pottery and rusted and tarnished metal looked particularly pathetic in the bright sunlight.

Sandra blinked. "That's it? What about gold coins? Jewelry? Silver."

"This flask is silver." He held up the small flask, which was black with tarnish. "It's even engraved, see?" He pointed to a faint pattern barely discernable through the black. "Something like this would have cost a good bit in its day. It might even have belonged to Passionata herself."

Sandra picked up one of the pieces of broken china. It was smaller than the palm of her hand and featured part of a painting of a bird. "This looks like something I'd throw in the trash."

Adam took the china from her. "This china is likely from a set specially commissioned by the British Royal Navy," he said. "If so, it's worth a fortune."

"Broken?" Sandra wrinkled her nose. "What else do you have?"

"That's it," Adam said. "At least until we can launch a full-scale salvage expedition."

Sandra turned to the camera man. "Get your underwater gear ready. We'll have to dive the wreck itself, see if we can get any decent footage there."

"The stuff that you can see underwater looks even worse." Nicole spoke for the first time since Ian's arrival on the ship. She'd avoided looking at him and had positioned herself on the opposite side of the deck, as far from her as possible. He'd spent most of his time staring at her, hoping to catch her looking his way. He had ten days to convince her he was sorry about deceiving her. Ten days to prove he loved her.

"It can't look much worse," Sandra said.

"Most of it is either buried in silt or covered in barnacles," Nicole said. "Not to mention the wreck is a favorite hangout of barracudas and sharks." She shook her head. "After what happened to Adam, you won't get me back down there."

Sandra was silent for a long moment, turning a broken bottle over and over in her hand. She couldn't ignore the fact that Adam *had* been attacked by a shark. And the prospect of risking injury for footage of barnacle-covered trash couldn't have been appealing.

"That's why we need the time to get funding to launch a professional expedition," Adam said. "We need robots, shark cages, cranes, cameras and a lot of sophisticated equipment and experienced people to salvage the ship safely and to keep the valuable artifacts as intact as possible."

She nodded, then raised her head to meet his eyes. "So you're telling me there's no story here. Not yet, anyway."

"That's right," he said. He nodded to the table of artifacts. "This stuff means a lot to a historian like me, but I doubt your viewers would be very excited about this version of a pirate's treasure."

She glanced at Nicole. "He's telling the truth?"

Nicole nodded. "He's telling the truth." And then she did look at Ian, when she said the word *truth.* As if he needed reminding how much the concept meant to her.

Sandra turned to Adam. "I'm willing to leave, on one condition."

He looked wary. "What's that?"

"You keep me posted and when you get ready for the actual salvage mission, I get the film rights to that."

"So when I come back to the island, not only will I have to deal with sharks, barracudas and the financier's bean counters, I'll have to put up with you?"

She grinned. "Think of it as an added benefit."

"I'll give you the first option to buy the film rights to the salvage expedition," Adam said.

"It's a deal." She extended her hand, but when Adam took it, she surprised him by pulling him toward her and kissing his cheek. The others burst out laughing as he turned bright red, pink lip marks branded on the side of his face.

She pretended not to notice his embarrassment and turned briskly businesslike, ordering the cameraman back to the ship. "We'll leave first thing tomorrow," she said. "It was a pleasure meeting you all." She shook Nicole's hand. "I think you're smart to stay away from that one," she said, nodding to Adam. "He needs a woman as stubborn as he is to keep him in line."

"Hey, I resent that!" Adam protested.

Sandra turned next to Ian. She took his hand and squeezed it. "I have a lot of footage of the island you can have if you think it will help FREE and their cause."

This generous offer surprised him. Maybe there was some softness beneath Sandra's steely exterior. "Thanks," he said. "That would be great."

"I'll send it to you in London. After all, I have your address."

They said their final goodbyes, then she was gone. They were all silent, watching her departure. "She didn't make a very good first impression on me," Nicole said finally. "But given enough time, I think I might actually grow to like her."

"I haven't changed my mind about her at all," Adam said. "I wouldn't trust a thing she said. My goal from now on is to stay as far away from her as possible."

"That might be tough if she films the salvage expedition," Ian said.

Adam grunted and stalked off, disappearing into the cabin. Ian looked at Nicole, who stood a few feet away, still staring out at the water as if he wasn't there.

As if he had no place in her life anymore.

He couldn't let things go on like this. He'd had a sleepless night to think about everything that had happened, all he'd done and said. Yes, he'd been wrong to deceive Nicole and to hurt her, but his sin wasn't great enough to deserve the punishment she meted out. He would allow her to take the lead in everything but this.

Maybe being a real man didn't have anything to do with hacking a living out of the wilderness or being able to lift so many pounds or engaging in sexual exploits or macho posturing. Maybe what counted most was being honest with others, and with himself, about who he was and what he wanted. And what he wanted most was to love Nicole and to be with her.

Nicole felt Ian watching her, and fought the urge to turn and throw herself into his arms. She might not be Passionata, but she was no weakling, either. She had to find a middle ground— a way to clear the air between them without a complete surrender.

He moved closer to her. "Nicole, I know I hurt you," he began. "And I never meant to do that. I hope one day you'll forgive me."

She turned toward him at last, her hands clinging to the deck rail behind her, both to hold herself up and to keep from reaching for him. "I've been doing a lot of thinking," she said. "While I still believe you were wrong to lie to me, I see now you weren't the only person practicing deception here."

He frowned. "What do you mean?"

"I came on pretty strong the first night we were together, remember?"

He smiled, desire reflected in his eyes. "I'll never forget."

Her skin prickled with the memory of his touch and she clung more tightly to the railing. "I was inspired by Passionata's autobiography to try new things. To be more assertive. Frankly, you were an experiment."

He chuckled. "I was a willing guinea pig. And it's not as if your experiments were unenjoyable."

"Right. But what I'm getting at is, I'm not usually like that. Before, I've always been rather…passive in relationships."

"People change. I can't see you ever being passive again." His smile was suggestive. "At least, not all the time."

Heat curled through her middle and she had trouble staying focused on the words she'd planned to say. "You're probably right, but I'm not a ball breaker like Sandra, either."

"Thank God for that," he murmured.

A nervous laugh escaped her. "You aren't making this easy."

His expression sobered. "I'm sorry. Go on."

"All right." She took a deep breath. "Do you love me?" She'd decided the direct question was the only way to approach this—one lesson she'd learned from Passionata.

He didn't hesitate to answer. "I do. I never expected it, but it happened."

Her spirits lifted at his words, in spite of the doubts that remained. She forged on. "I have to know. Did you fall in love with *me,* or with the woman I was pretending to be?"

He studied her a long moment, then spoke slowly, as if weighing each word. "Love isn't something that happens only in bed. I fell in love with the wild woman who commanded me to satisfy her sexually. But I also fell in love with the woman swimming beside me, and the woman I sat across from at meals, and the one who walked beside me on the beach. All of those women are part of you." He touched her cheek. "And I love them all."

She was melting now, so close to giving in and throwing her arms around him, but there was more she needed to say. "I'm glad you see all of me—the good and the bad. I've never been quite so clear-sighted when it came to love. I don't think I realized until just now, when I watched Sandra with Adam's treasure."

"What do you mean?"

She smiled weakly. "Sandra and I may be different in a lot of ways, but I realized we had one thing in common. We both had expectations of something glamorous and beautiful and dazzling—the stuff of fantasy. And we were both disappointed. For her, it was the treasure. For me, it was a relationship."

She let go of the railing and put one hand on his arm, craving that physical connection. "Maybe real love is like real treasure—tarnished and flawed at times, but no less valuable."

"I may be a boring academic, but you're worth more to me than any dusty artifacts or rare plant species." He pulled her close. "And if you have any flaws, they only make you more beautiful and perfect for a flawed guy like me."

She answered him with a kiss, and for a long time the only communication between them was the kind that needed no words. Being back in his arms was like coming home again—so safe and secure. So right.

When at last they drew apart, she smiled up at him. "I love you," she said.

"I love you, too." He grinned. "How would you like to come to England with me when we're done on this island?"

"I'd like that."

"My apartment has plenty of room for two, and I'm thinking there are a few things from Passionata's book we haven't tried yet," he teased.

"There might be," she said. "I'd better get my whip and handcuffs and start practicing."

"I'll work on my groveling."

She laughed. "No groveling for you. That's one thing the pirate queen definitely got wrong. Things work best for men and women when they love as equals."

"I couldn't agree more." They kissed again, and Nicole surrendered to the magical, floating feeling of being in love. She'd come to Passionata's island hoping to figure out her life. She'd found more than she bargained for. Adam wasn't the only one leaving here with a treasure, and hers was truly priceless.

* * * * *

Turn the page for a sneak preview of
AFTERSHOCK, *a new anthology*
featuring New York Times *bestselling author*
Sharon Sala.

Available October 2008.

n ● c t u r n e™

Dramatic and sensual tales of paranormal romance.

Chapter 1

October
New York City

Nicole Masters was sitting cross-legged on her sofa while a cold autumn rain peppered the windows of her fourth-floor apartment. She was poking at the ice cream in her bowl and trying not to be in a mood.

Six weeks ago, a simple trip to her neighborhood pharmacy had turned into a nightmare. She'd walked into the middle of a robbery. She never even saw the man who shot her in the head and left her for dead. She'd survived, but some of her senses had not. She was dealing with short-term memory loss and a tendency to stagger. Even though she'd been told the problems were most likely temporary, she waged a daily battle with depression.

Her parents had been killed in a car wreck when she was twenty-one. And except for a few friends—and most recently her boyfriend, Dominic Tucci, who lived in the apartment right above hers, she was alone. Her doctor kept reminding her that she should be grateful to be alive, and on one level she knew he was right. But he wasn't living in her shoes.

If she'd been anywhere else but at that pharmacy when the robbery happened, she wouldn't have died twice on the way to the hospital. Instead of being grateful that she'd survived, she couldn't stop thinking of what she'd lost.

But that wasn't the end of her troubles. On top of everything else, something strange was happening inside her head. She'd begun to hear odd things: sounds, not voices—at least, she didn't think it was voices. It was more like the distant noise of rapids— a rush of wind and water inside her head that, when it came, blocked out everything around her. It didn't happen often, but when it did, it was frightening, and it was driving her crazy.

The blank moments, which is what she called them, even had a rhythm. First there came that sound, then a cold sweat, then panic with no reason. Part of her feared it was the beginning of an emotional breakdown. And part of her feared it wasn't—that it was going to turn out to be a permanent souvenir of her resurrection.

Frustrated with herself and the situation as it stood, she upped the sound on the TV remote. But instead of *Wheel of Fortune,* an announcer broke in with a special bulletin.

"This just in. Police are on the scene of a kidnapping that occurred only hours ago at The Dakota. Molly Dane, the six-year-old daughter of one of Hollywood's blockbuster stars, Lyla Dane, was taken by force from the family apartment. At this time they have yet to receive a ransom demand. The housekeeper was seriously injured during the abduction, and is, at the present time, in surgery. Police are hoping to be able to talk to her once she regains consciousness. In the meantime, we are going now to a press conference with Lyla Dane."

Horrified, Nicole stilled as the cameras went live to where the actress was speaking before a bank of microphones. The shock and terror in Lyla Dane's voice were physically painful to watch. But even though Nicole kept upping the volume, the sound continued to fade.

Just when she was beginning to think something was wrong with her set, the broadcast suddenly switched from the Dane press conference to what appeared to be footage of the kidnapping, beginning with footage from inside the apartment.

When the front door suddenly flew back against the wall and four men rushed in, Nicole gasped. Horrified, she quickly realized that this must have been caught on a security camera inside the Dane apartment.

As Nicole continued to watch, a small Asian woman, who she guessed was the maid, rushed forward in an effort to keep them out. When one of the men hit her in the face with his gun, Nicole moaned. The violence was too reminiscent of what she'd lived through. Sick to her stomach, she fisted her hands against her belly, wishing it was over, but unable to tear her gaze away.

When the maid dropped to the carpet, the same man followed with a vicious kick to the little woman's midsection that lifted her off the floor.

"Oh, my God," Nicole said. When blood began to pool beneath the maid's head, she started to cry.

As the tape played on, the four men split up in different directions. The camera caught one running down a long marble hallway, then disappearing into a room. Moments later he reappeared, carrying a little girl, who Nicole assumed was Molly Dane. The child was wearing a pair of red pants and a white turtleneck sweater, and her hair was partially blocking her abductor's face as he carried her down the hall. She was kicking and screaming in his arms, and when he slapped her, it elicited an agonized scream that brought the other three running. Nicole watched in horror as one of them ran up and put his hand over Molly's face. Seconds later, she went limp.

One moment they were in the foyer, then they were gone.

Nicole jumped to her feet, then staggered drunkenly. The bowl of ice cream she'd absentmindedly placed in her lap shattered at her feet, splattering glass and melting ice cream everywhere.

The picture on the screen abruptly switched from the kidnapping to what Nicole assumed was a rerun of Lyla Dane's plea for her daughter's safe return, but she was numb.

Before she could think what to do next, the doorbell rang. Startled by the unexpected sound, she shakily swiped at the tears and took a step forward. She didn't feel the glass shards piercing her feet until she took the second step. At that point, sharp pains shot through her foot. She gasped, then looked down in confusion. Her legs looked as if she'd been running through mud, and she was standing in broken glass and ice cream, while a thin ribbon of blood seeped out from beneath her toes.

"Oh, no," Nicole mumbled, then stifled a second moan of pain.

The doorbell rang again. She shivered, then clutched her head in confusion.

"Just a minute!" she yelled, then tried to sidestep the rest of the debris as she hobbled to the door.

When she looked through the peephole in the door, she didn't know whether to be relieved or regretful.

It was Dominic, and as usual, she was a mess.

Nicole smiled a little self-consciously as she opened the door to let him in. "I just don't know what's happening to me. I think I'm losing my mind."

"Hey, don't talk about my woman like that."

Nicole rode the surge of delight his words brought. "So I'm still your woman?"

Dominic lowered his head.

Their lips met.

The kiss proceeded.

Slowly.

Thoroughly.

* * * * *

Be sure to look for the AFTERSHOCK *anthology next month, as well as other exciting paranormal stories from Silhouette Nocturne. Available in October wherever books are sold.*

Silhouette®

SPECIAL EDITION™

FROM *NEW YORK TIMES* BESTSELLING AUTHOR

LINDA LAEL MILLER

A STONE CREEK CHRISTMAS

Veterinarian Olivia O'Ballivan finds the animals in Stone Creek playing Cupid between her and Tanner Quinn. Even Tanner's daughter, Sophie, is eager to play matchmaker. With everyone conspiring against them and the holiday season fast approaching, Tanner and Olivia may just get everything they want for Christmas after all!

Available December 2008 wherever books are sold.

Harlequin® Historical
Historical Romantic Adventure!

HALLOWE'EN HUSBANDS

With three fantastic stories by

Lisa Plumley
Denise Lynn
Christine Merrill

Don't miss these unforgettable
stories about three women who
experience the mysterious
happenings of Allhallows Eve
and come to discover that finding
true love on this eerie day is not
so scary after all.

Look for
HALLOWE'EN HUSBANDS

Available October
wherever books are sold.

Silhouette®

Romantic
SUSPENSE

**Sparked by Danger,
Fueled by Passion.**

USA TODAY bestselling author

Merline Lovelace

Undercover Wife

Secret agent Mike Callahan, code name Hawkeye,
objects when he's paired with sophisticated
Gillian Ridgeway on a dangerous spy mission
to Hong Kong. Gillian has secretly been in love
with him for years, but Hawk is an overprotective
man with a wounded past that threatens to
resurface. Now the two must put their lives—
and hearts—at risk for each other.

Available October wherever books are sold.

REQUEST YOUR FREE BOOKS!

2 FREE NOVELS PLUS 2 FREE GIFTS!

HARLEQUIN®

Blaze™

Red-hot reads!

YES! Please send me 2 FREE Harlequin® Blaze™ novels and my 2 FREE gifts (gifts are worth about $10). After receiving them, if I don't wish to receive any more books, I can return the shipping statement marked "cancel". If I don't cancel, I will receive 6 brand-new novels every month and be billed just $4.24 per book in the U.S. or $4.71 per book in Canada, plus 25¢ shipping and handling per book and applicable taxes, if any*. That's a savings of 15% or more off the cover price! I understand that accepting the 2 free books and gifts places me under no obligation to buy anything. I can always return a shipment and cancel at any time. Even if I never buy another book, the two free books and gifts are mine to keep forever.

151 HDN ERVA   351 HDN ERUX

Name	(PLEASE PRINT)	
Address		Apt. #
City	State/Prov.	Zip/Postal Code

Signature (if under 18, a parent or guardian must sign)

Mail to the Harlequin Reader Service:
IN U.S.A.: P.O. Box 1867, Buffalo, NY 14240-1867
IN CANADA: P.O. Box 609, Fort Erie, Ontario L2A 5X3

Not valid to current subscribers of Harlequin Blaze books.

Want to try two free books from another line?
Call 1-800-873-8635 or visit www.morefreebooks.com.

* Terms and prices subject to change without notice. N.Y. residents add applicable sales tax. Canadian residents will be charged applicable provincial taxes and GST. Offer not valid in Quebec. This offer is limited to one order per household. All orders subject to approval. Credit or debit balances in a customer's account(s) may be offset by any other outstanding balance owed by or to the customer. Please allow 4 to 6 weeks for delivery. Offer available while quantities last.

Your Privacy: Harlequin Books is committed to protecting your privacy. Our Privacy Policy is available online at www.eHarlequin.com or upon request from the Reader Service. From time to time we make our lists of customers available to reputable third parties who may have a product or service of interest to you. If you would prefer we not share your name and address, please check here. ☐

HB08R

HARLEQUIN®

Blaze™

COMING NEXT MONTH

#423 LETHAL EXPOSURE Lori Wilde
Perfect Anatomy, Bk. 3
Wanting to expand her sexual IQ, Julie DeMarco selects Sebastian Black—hotshot PR exec—to participate in a no-strings fling. The playboy should be an easygoing love-'em-and-leave-'em type, but what if there's more to the man than just his good looks?

#424 MS. MATCH Jo Leigh
The Wrong Bed
Oops! It's the wrong sister! Paul Bennet agrees to take plain Jane Gwen Christopher on a charity date only to score points with her gorgeous sister. So what is he thinking when he wakes up beside Gwen the very next morning?

#425 AMOROUS LIAISONS Sarah Mayberry
Lust in Translation
Max Laurent thought he was over his attraction to Maddy Green. But when she shows up on the doorstep of his Paris flat, it turns out the lust never went away. He's determined to stay silent so as not to ruin their friendship—until the night she seduces him, that is.

#426 GOOD TO THE LAST BITE Crystal Green
Vampire Edward Marburn has only one goal left—to take vengeance on Gisele, the female vamp who'd stolen his humanity. Before long, Edward has Gisele right where he wants her. And he learns that the joys of sexual revenge can last an eternity....

#427 HER SECRET TREASURE Cindi Myers
Adam Carroway never thought he'd agree to work with Sandra Newman. Hit the sheets with her...absolutely. But work together? Still, his expedition needs the publicity her TV show will bring. Besides, what could be sexier than working out their differences in bed?

#428 WATCH AND LEARN Stephanie Bond
Sex for Beginners, Bk. 1
When recently divorced Gemma Jacobs receives a letter she'd written to herself ten years ago in college, she never guesses the contents will inspire her to take charge of her sexuality, to unleash her forbidden exhibitionist tendencies...and to seduce her totally hot, voyeuristic new neighbor....

www.eHarlequin.com

HBCNM0908